under the wolf, under the dog

under the wolf, under the dog

ADAM RAPP

CANDLEWICK PRESS
CAMBRIDGE, MASSACHUSETTS

Copyright © 2004 by Adam Rapp

First edition 2004

Library of Congress Cataloging-in-Publication Data

Rapp, Adam.
Under the wolf, under the dog / Adam Rapp. —1st ed.
p. cm.
Summary: Sixteen-year-old Steve struggles to make sense of his mother's terminal breast cancer and his brother's suicide.
ISBN 0-7636-1818-7
[1. Depression, Mental—Fiction. 2. Family problems—Fiction.
3. Grief—Fiction. 4. Drug abuse—Fiction. 5. Suicide—Fiction.
6. Cancer—Fiction. 7. Death—Fiction. 8. Illinois—Fiction.] I. Title.
PZ7.R18133Un 2004
[Fic]—dc22   2004050255

2 4 6 8 10 9 7 5 3 1

Printed in the United States of America

This book was typeset in Granjon.

Candlewick Press
2067 Massachusetts Avenue
Cambridge, Massachusetts 02140

visit us at www.candlewick.com

For K. V.

A Pretty Depressing Time in My Life

by Steve Nugent

1.

How to start.

Okay. Here it goes.

Mrs. Leene said I should begin by describing myself.

So, my name is Steve Nugent. I'm just seventeen. It was my birthday last month, in November. Now it's the middle of December, and the trees around here are caked in ice and sort of silvery in that creepy, wintry way, so right now seventeen seems like a hundred years off.

Where I'm from, they call me White Steve because I'm so pale. The ones who call me that are pale too, but not as pale as me. I'm like soap or paper. I'm like Easter candy. I'm like glue or piano keys. If I stay in the sun too long, I turn pink; not red—*pink,* like Spam.

In terms of size, I'm six foot three and about 145 pounds, which is way too skinny, I know. I can't help that right now. The doctors say I'll fill out in a few years. At this point I would describe myself as being a pretty high-percentage dodge-ball target.

I guess my hair is brown, but there might be some red in it, which makes me worry about my future pubic situation—as in when I finally get some upholstery down low, what color it will be.

That might be too much information.

Sorry.

I'm also blind in my right eye, which I will tell you more about later.

I'm from East Foote, which is on the Illinois side of the Mississippi. Foote is on the Iowa side, and it's about ten times the size of East Foote. To put it in perspective, before I left, most people in East Foote had to go stand on this old livestock promontory just to get cell phone reception.

So I'm currently in residence at this place in the middle of Michigan called Burnstone Grove. There are about thirty-five kids here. About half of us are drug addicts, and the other half have tried to check out of this world in one way or another. Probably a third of us have dabbled in both pursuits. I don't entirely fit into either category, so I'm what they call a Gray Grouper. The Red Groupers are the junkies, and the Blue Groupers are the suicide kids. There are only seven Gray Groupers, and we're generally kept here for a month or two before we're either shipped back home or sent to another, more affordable, facility. The Red and Blue Groupers can stay here for over a year sometimes. They get to see the seasons change and everything. So far it's been nothing but snow and ice and frozen trees and this very low-looking iron sky.

The truth is that I could easily be a Red or Blue Grouper. I've done some drugs, and I have to admit that I've thought about the other scenario more than once. All of that will come later, though. I don't want to tell you everything just yet.

It's Christmas break, so we don't have to go to classes. We still have to do group and one-on-one counseling and stuff like that. I have a few weeks off, so I thought this would be a good time to start this thing.

A girl on the second floor who they call Silent Starla is here because she tried to kill herself with kitchen cleanser. I have no idea how that works exactly, but that's what they say about her. She wears Chicago Cubs wristbands, but she's sort of goth and hip-hop at the same time, which is really hard to explain correctly. I can't really figure her out, but I must confess that she intrigues me.

There's this homosexual here from Detroit named Rory Parker. He's what they call a bug-chaser, which means he only sleeps with men who are infected with

AIDS. He stays on the fourth floor, and his parents are said to be the wealthiest family in the state of Michigan. Apparently he's been trying to get HIV for like three years now. He's a Blue Grouper and wears so much black eyeliner he looks like he works at a haunted house or something.

There's this Red Grouper down the hall from me named Shannon Lynch who can stick $1.87 in change up his nose. It's pretty amazing. He gets like four quarters, a bunch of dimes, and a few nickels all the way up it. He's from the western suburbs of Chicago, and he's been here for three months. He had a pretty bad problem with heroin—he was shooting it and everything. His parents dropped him off three months ago, and he's been clean ever since. He's one of four Red Groupers on this new methadone program for teens that they just instituted called Mindful Methadone. He told me that they mix the stuff with Tang and that it has a pretty bitter aftertaste.

In my opinion, Shannon Lynch is the coolest person at Burnstone Grove. He wears this old jean jacket buttoned all the way up and pretty much keeps to himself. Besides the change-up-the-nose thing, what's cool about him is that he is a trained cellist—as in he spent a year at this special conservatory in Cleveland and everything—but he listens to punk rock, like old Sex

Pistols and Meters. He also knows a lot about Shakespeare and Sam Shepard. He says he wants to be a stage actor. He's currently reading this book called *The Theatre and Its Double,* by Antonin Artaud. He nods a little when he reads it. Most people who nod like that when they read can't pull that kind of thing off. I genuinely hope things work out for Shannon.

So I'm writing all of this down because Mrs. Leene, my lead counselor, thought it would be good for me. I haven't been able to say much in group, which is short for group therapy, although I'm sure you already knew that. To be honest, I haven't said one word in group yet. I pretty much just sit on my hands and listen to everyone else. I guess I'm sort of introverted. Or maybe it's a combination of shyness and boredom. At my first Gray Group meeting, the seven of us had to pick one other person and use one positive word to describe him or her. This girl named Amanda Pelt said I was "pensive," which made me try to seem anti-pensive for like three days after that, like I'd walk around trying to *not* think and constantly de-furrow my brow and that kind of thing. But that just led to a general feeling of anxiety and dried out my eyes for some reason, and then I pretty much felt like holing up in my room and picking my cuticles.

Amanda Pelt was born in Pacific Palisades, which

is in some weird part of Los Angeles, and then moved to Green Bay, Wisconsin, after her dad died in his sleep. She apparently has these really high SAT scores but has a severe problem with feeling anything, so she does things like slam her hand in silverware drawers and stuff like that. She has really pretty blue eyes. One day a few weeks ago, I thought I was in love with her, but when I sat next to her in the cafeteria, she told me to get away from her.

"Go away," she said.

"Sorry," I said.

"Don't be sorry. Just get the fuck away from me."

Yeah, that was pretty harsh.

I haven't thought about her in the same way since.

Mrs. Leene calls this whole writing thing bibliotherapy, which sounds pretty intimidating if you ask me. By the time anyone reads this, hopefully I'll be out of this place and on to better things.

So a couple of months ago, my brother, Welton, hanged himself with a necktie.

I think that's a good place to begin.

My mom died just a few weeks before that, and I wasn't particularly excited about much.

At the wake they kept his casket open. I know I was probably supposed to be thinking about a lot of important stuff like life and death and the hereafter, but for some reason I was preoccupied by looking for bruises around my brother's throat. In all honesty there wasn't much to see because the funeral home did a pretty thorough makeup job.

When my cousin Grace caught me touching Welton's Adam's apple, I got an erection; I'm not sure why. Grace is pretty, but relatives aren't supposed to be able to have that effect on you. She looked directly at me, and my face got so hot, I thought my eyes would burst. I had to walk back to my seat with my hands clasped in front of my slacks like I was praying.

For some reason, during the hymns I kept seeing Jesus with an erection, too—like up there on the cross with all those ribs and his big holy member. That scared me a little.

Over the St. Rose of East Foote's confessionals there's this huge stained-glass window. On the other side looms an ancient maple tree whose shadow trembles on the glass like a witch's hand. It was like ninety-five degrees that day, and the church fans weren't doing much more than pushing the hot air around. I was imagining myself up in the crotch of that maple tree, watching everybody looking grave and bereft and holding back the tears, wondering if anyone was curious about where I was. I know that's selfish, but I couldn't help it; it's where my mind goes sometimes.

After Welton's funeral, a bunch of my overweight relatives went bowling. My aunt Ricky organized it because she thought it would keep everyone's spirits up. Aunt Ricky's really into bowling and bingo and family potlucks and all that. I blew it off and went home and sat on the toilet for a few hours. I guess I wasn't feeling particularly sporty that day.

No one knows why Welton did it. Welton's my older brother, by the way. Or *was* my older brother.

When I think about it now, I'm not sure if Welton would have been a Red Grouper or a Blue Grouper. He was sort of both, if you want to know the truth. They would have had to combine colors for him and start a Purple Group.

I just realized that a grouper is a fish. In the Burnstone Grove library dictionary, it says it's "any of various often large food and game fishes of the genera *Epinephelus.*" I wonder if that's how the faculty here thinks of us all—as a school of oversize, deeply troubled walking fish.

The weird thing about the library is that the Blue Groupers aren't allowed to check out hardcover books because it's supposed to be somehow possible to kill yourself with them. I can't picture that. Maybe with a corner or something.

So Welton and my mom weren't that close.

My mom my mom my mom my mom my mom . . .

They actually fought a lot because Welton had problems in school. He cut classes a lot and smoked pot during free periods and got suspended once for turning in an illegal term paper on *The Canterbury Tales* that he'd purchased off the Internet. Besides basketball, what he was really good at was drawing things. He could pretty much perfectly sketch anything he saw, but he stopped doing it around the age of thirteen after he came home from this art camp in Des Moines with poison ivy and chigger bites.

My mom always urged him to develop his artistic skill, but all Welton wanted to do was play basketball and run around with his burnout friends at night. I always thought it was strange that he was a jock and a druggie—that's not your everyday combination. Once my dad caught him huffing model airplane glue, but he sort of turned a blind eye. He walked in on him in the bathroom, and Welton was inhaling the fumes from the bottom of a brown paper bag. I was in the hallway, on my way to the kitchen.

"What are you doing?" my dad asked him.

"Nothing," Welton answered, and crumpled the bag.

My dad stood there for a moment and said, "Be good, okay, son?"

"Okay," Welton said.

Neither of them knew I saw that.

Maybe Welton killed himself because he lived in the basement. Who knows what all that damp air and cement will do to a person? Down there there's nothing but the washer and dryer and unwanted books and Welton's BMX mag wheels and my old Green Machine and my dad's kayak that he never uses and a folded-up Ping-Pong table and boxes of Christmas ornaments and photo albums and report cards and ancient, glued-shut Advent calendars and basically all types of other things that are easier to forget about if they're stuffed away somewhere.

Maybe he killed himself because for the last year of his life all he did was smoke weed, play Vice City on his PlayStation II, and listen to Bottomside's "Forty Holes and Forty Goals" on permanent replay.

As a junior, Welton was the starting small forward on the East Foote varsity basketball team, but he had to quit three-quarters of the way through the season because of a herniated disk. He had this condition called sciatica, which almost crippled him. If he stood for more than two minutes at a time, the backs of his legs would start aching so bad he'd have to sit down. They were going to perform invasive surgery to fuse his vertebrae, but one of my mom's friends whose husband had suffered from the same condition convinced her to make Welton wait it out, to see if the bulge would somehow go away. Fortunately for Welton, it did—the doctor said it was a small miracle—but my brother never quite made it back onto the basketball court.

The other day I was reading about these dogs called salukis that have to run or they'll die of depression. I'm not suggesting that my parents had canine genes or anything, but maybe through some process of karmic evolution, Welton had some saluki in him. Maybe when he stopped playing ball, something shut down and could never get rebooted.

This Blue Grouper from the second floor told Shannon Lynch that we've all been animals in former lives. The guy's name is Jimmy Smallhorn and he has a permanent facial tick and he's from the Upper Peninsula—a Uper, they call him. He told Shannon that he was a wolf in his past life and that sometimes he can feel his former wolfness creeping into his thoughts. I try to stay away from that guy.

And then again, maybe it was some weird noise in my brother's head, some little digital murmur he never told anyone about. I've heard about that—how you wake up one day and there's like this permanent dial tone droning somewhere behind the meat in your head, a little Dustbuster trapped where the brain saves you from going crazy. After a while you wind up ending it all just to make things quiet again.

I found Welton in his room in the basement. He'd knotted the necktie around a hook at the top of his door. The hook had broken, but that didn't stop the asphyxiation. What's weird is that he was kneeling. It looked like he was praying or pulling up weeds in a garden.

His TV was blaring applause from *The Price Is Right*. An old Hispanic woman named Carmelita had just won the Showcase Showdown, and she was so excited she practically body-slammed Bob Barker. Why I can remember that woman's name, I have no idea. It's weird how those random details will stick in your head.

For some reason Welton was nude and half his face was blue. Right now when I close my eyes and try and see the parts of his body, I keep missing stuff, like his arms and his shoulders. I can see his face as clear as day and I could even go into detail about his Adam's apple or this little blue vein under his right eye or the weird paste that was coming out of his left nostril, but other more obvious things like limbs are lost to me. Limbs and eye color. I can't place that either. It was like someone had stolen that stuff.

Once I overheard this old man at the Foote dog track telling someone that when greyhounds die, they ship them off to a special factory in Mexico and grind them up and turn them into model airplane glue. For some reason, for the past week or so I keep imagining Welton as a little tube of glue. Mrs. Leene thinks it's part of the process of dealing with death, that we have to somehow *objectify* the ones we lose in order to let go of them. I'm not sure about that. It seems a little easy and logical.

When my dad saw Welton's death pose, he just sat on the bed and fluffed a pillow, like he wanted to go to sleep or something.

I was like, "Dad . . . Dad," but he just kept fluffing the pillow.

The EMT guys were as quiet as aliens, and when they pushed the gurney through the living room, I finally reached over and closed Welton's mouth.

"Bye," I said to him as they wheeled him away.

Just for a second I had the feeling that he might say something back, but he didn't. He just looked sort of waxy and stunned.

My dad had to fill out a bunch of forms. He didn't ask any questions, and when the ambulance pulled away, it was like they were hauling away a piece of furniture, like Welton was a table or a grandfather clock or something. I know my mom would have been making coffee for everyone and trying not to cry—she was strong like that—but she was already dead, and like so many things in our kitchen, our coffeemaker had lost its purpose.

The cops were even quieter than the ambulance people. There were two of them and they had identical mustaches and I kept thinking they were lovers. My dad had to fill out yet another report and answer even more questions, and after a few friendly squeezes on my shoulder, they left with such ease it was as if they'd stopped by to drop off a bushel of apples.

The last thing Welton told me was that Lincoln was a better president than Washington. I have no idea why he said that or what it was supposed to mean. It was the middle of the night and he was standing naked in front of my bedroom door and he was totally wasted.

"Lincoln was a better president, Steve," he said. His testicles were dangling all huge and lazy.

I was like, "Better than who?"

"Better than Washington."

"Oh," I said.

"You can tell 'cause of the pictures," he added. "His beard and stuff."

2

My room is colder than usual.

Last night I had to pull the covers off the other bed. Not that that matters much, seeing as no one is actually sleeping in it. I am currently the only Gray Grouper without a roommate.

I wonder if the people at Burnstone Grove make it colder on purpose. To somehow regulate us or whatever.

Don't get me wrong—I don't live in a cell. I have a sink with running water and a pretty decent bed and electricity and a closet and this rose-colored carpeting, and the things in my room are made out of real wood—it really isn't all that bad. And I do have a window, too, which overlooks a stand of fir trees that are currently shaggy with snow.

So this isn't some third-world like *hovel* or whatever; it really isn't.

Yesterday Shannon lent me a CD by this band called Interpol. I fell asleep listening to a song called

"Stella Was a Diver and She Was Always Down." I couldn't understand all of the lyrics, but it's a pretty good song.

I was told earlier today that I might get a roommate within the next week or two. They didn't tell me anything about him. I hope he's cool and not some psycho Blue Grouper from like Flint or someplace.

The other day they finally took the rail off the foot of my bed. I was having to sleep with my legs all bunched up and I was getting these crazy cramps in the middle of the night. Now I can finally stretch out and sleep like a regular human.

"Tell me more about your brother," Mrs. Leene said to me during our session this morning. She made it a point to tell me about how I tend to get sleepy whenever the subject of Welton comes up. She said that phenomenon's called "conflict narcolepsy," which would make a pretty interesting band name if you think about it.

But before I begin, I must confess that I think Mrs. Leene is sort of hot. I know she's in her forties and old enough to be my mother, but I can't help it. She has these big brown eyes and nice wet lips.

Okay.

Enough of that.

So my brother . . .

For most of the last year of his life, Welton worked

at a nursing home where he and this guy named Dantly would steal medication. As I already said, he was definitely half Red Grouper. Dantly, however, is a hundred percent Red Grouper. That guy will take anything. I saw him eat a light bulb once and I'm not kidding. He smashed it with a hammer and put all the glass between two slices of Wonder bread and ate it like a sandwich. And nothing happened. He just burped and then jumped over this fence and tackled my brother. Dantly's a freak through and through. A total burnout. Half shark. A quarter invincible. Maybe even part machine. Instead of blood, the guy probably has motor oil coursing through his veins. He and my brother mostly took this drug called Haldol, which according to Welton makes you feel like you're half-asleep in a snowdrift.

My brother was eventually fired from the nursing home because he got caught leaving the grounds with a potted poinsettia. That's kind of funny if you think about it—a drug addict getting busted for stealing a holiday plant. Welton told me later that he was planning to grow marijuana in the planter, that Dantly had already ripped off these special UV lamps from the high school science lab and that they were hiding them at this condemned building over in the Foote warehouse district.

So the thing that screws me up the most, I think, is our basement.

Welton stopped coming upstairs after he lost his job at the nursing home. Every so often you would hear him shuffling around. The basement toilet would flush or a door would close, and that would be his way of talking to us.

"Was that Welton?" my dad would ask.

"Yeah, that was him," I'd say.

My dad, Richard Nugent, manages and half owns a secondhand electronics shop on the other side of the river. It's mostly microwaves and clock radios and other totally unnecessary household appliances. He used to go for only vintage stuff, like old Victrola record players, but it eventually turned into a kind of modern swap shop.

My dad started watching a lot of TV after my mom got sick. Lyman Singer, my dad's business partner, insisted that he take some time off so he could spend more time at home, but I don't think it did my dad any good. All he did was gorge himself on health cereal and watch sitcoms. And he passed gas about every twelve seconds, too. There's nothing like your dad farting you out of your own living room.

Once that previous winter, after my mom got diagnosed, I came home and he was wearing a swimsuit. It was December and the house was freezing. He was sitting in his chair, watching a rerun of *Malcolm in the Middle.* The studio audience was laughing so hard it sounded like they'd been bribed.

"Dad, what are you doing?" I asked.

"Goin' swimmin'," he said.

I said, "Dad, it's like twelve below. The river's totally frozen."

"There's ways around that," he said, and kept staring at the TV.

Yeah, he was pretty depressed, now that I think about it.

I was afraid that he actually *was* going to try to swim the river, so for the rest of *Malcolm in the Middle,* I sat on the sofa with my coat zipped. It got so cold you could see your own breath curling through the Magnavox light.

My dad eventually got up and went into his room. I thought I heard him crying, but when I pressed my ear to his door, the noise turned out to be a commercial on his clock radio about a ten-dollar all-you-can-eat buffet special at some restaurant in Monson.

Another time I came home from school and he was naked. He was watching this old sitcom from the seventies called *Three's Company,* and there were three cereal bowls at his feet. He was all skinny and sad like one of those totally defeated-looking guys you see in concentration camp pictures.

I was like, "Dad, you're naked."

He didn't even look up.

For some reason, I kept trying to see how much pubic hair he had. It was all matted and kind of orange, like something you use to scrub soap scum. When he caught me looking, he told me that the landlord on the show—Mr. Furley or whatever his name was—didn't try hard enough.

"That guy doesn't try hard enough, Steve," he said.

I felt weirdly ashamed when he said that. So much so that I went into his room and urinated on his bed.

I don't know why I did that.

I know this is supposed to be about my brother, but I guess it's about my dad, too.

3

So before I came to Burnstone Grove, I was going to this special school because of my math ability.

There are only like twenty kids in each grade and just about everybody is rich, and the few who aren't are so ridiculously smart it doesn't even matter. The place is called the East Foote School for the Gifted.

As a freshman at the regular East Foote high school, I got put in this advanced math class and I did well, so this guidance counselor called my parents and told them I was "percentile elite."

My mom hung up the phone and cried to my dad, "He's percentile elite, Dick!"

She was overjoyed and animated.

To me she shouted, "Steven, honey, you're percentile elite!"

After that, she looked into the gifted school and found out that I would qualify for some low-income scholarship, and so that's where I spent the past two years.

The gifted school is this little brick building on a hill overlooking this enormous cornfield that seems to go on for infinity. It's mostly populated by these totally nerdy-looking, antisocial geniuses with terrible eyesight. I'm not saying that I'm any better-looking, given how skinny and pale I am and how my voice still hasn't changed—in some ways I'm as nerdy as it goes—but the prodigies at the gifted school are all pocket-protectored-out and dressed by their nannies. The few who are even halfway normal-looking are so supremely stuck up they can hardly stand themselves.

Most of the gifted school graduates wind up going to MIT or Harvard or one of those places on the East Coast where the skyscrapers look like they're full of some dark, evil liquid.

At the end of my sophomore year, as part of this special program, I took the SATs and my scores were pretty high, so I started getting all these letters from Ivy League schools. I got really tired when I started looking at the brochures, though: nothing but fir trees and tennis courts and stone buildings with turrets and all of this other architecture that looks like it was built by the Catholic Church. I eventually threw most of that stuff out.

I don't understand why everyone makes such a big deal about SAT scores. Welton used to say that if you want to truly test somebody's intelligence, drop them in the middle of a jungle and give them like four matches, an unbreakable comb, and a rubber band and see how far they get. Throw a few wild beasts in there, too. Like a lion and a gorilla. There isn't a single kid at the gifted school who could survive something like that.

When my mom was still alive, she loved bringing up the subject of college. She really wanted me to go to a prestigious school and take charge of my future and *find myself* and all of that. Whenever she'd start lecturing, I'd wait for a lull and sneak out of her hospice room. It was easy because she was almost always falling asleep in the middle of a sentence. The morphine knocked her out pretty good. I know sneaking out of her hospice room isn't exactly being the model son or whatever, but the subject of higher education can turn just about anyone into an escape artist, trust me.

I've thought about the army, but I think all of the pushups and *Yes, sir*s and *No, sir*s would make me nervous.

To be perfectly honest, I wouldn't mind flying planes, but I've been told that I'm too tall for the air force. I know that I said I was six three, but I might actually be closer to six four. The only reason I say that is because the other day in the lounge, Shannon asked me in his sleepy voice, "Are you like six six, Steve?"

We were playing foosball, and he was pretty much handing my ass to me in a sling.

"No way," I said. "I'm not even six four."

"You're definitely six four," he said.

So maybe I am; I don't know. Lately my knees have been sore. The nurse here thinks I have this condition called Osgood-Schlatter, which is where the tissue under your patella tendon gets inflamed because you grow too fast.

When I was a freshman at EFHS, the junior varsity basketball coach kept stalking me to try out for the team. I know it was because of how Welton broke the single-season scoring record and made the all-conference team as a sophomore. The JV coach assumed that it ran in the family, and trust me, it doesn't. The only sport I've ever been good at is sleeping. I could win a gold medal in the Olympic sleeping marathon.

Welton was a legitimate six six. Just looking at him, you would have thought he was all slow and uncoordinated because of how he always slumped, but when he played basketball, something would come to life. He had like a thirty-five-inch vertical jump, and he could slam-dunk any way you wanted. The rim in our back-yard is so bent, you can't even play on it anymore.

The JV basketball coach eventually stopped stalking me after I standing-broad-jumped four-feet-some-thing for the Presidential Physical Fitness Test.

"Oh," he said when he wrote my pathetic distance on his clipboard.

Man, being tall is funny like that. Everyone wants you to play basketball or star in the school play or whatever. If I had my choice, I'd be like five two. Then the only people who would come after me would be the ones who'd want me to sack groceries or scrape rust off the bottoms of cars.

I should probably talk about Mary Mills a bit, because she certainly plays a part in the past several months.

"Have you ever had a girlfriend?" Mrs. Leene asked me the other day.

"No," I said. "Not really. There was this one girl, but . . ."

"But what?"

"I don't know."

"Tell me about her."

Then I started to tell her about Mary Mills. I tried, I really did—but just as I felt myself ready to launch into the whole drama, I sort of stopped talking and just sat there.

"Breathe, Steven," she said.

I couldn't breathe.

"You're not breathing, Steven. Settle down and breathe."

I settled down and breathed.

I definitely needed to do that.

"Are you okay?" she asked.

"I'm fine," I lied.

"Is this girl a source of embarrassment for you?"

"No," I lied again.

"Maybe you should write about her a little," she suggested.

So here it goes.

Mary Mills Mary Mills Mary Mills Mary Mills.

Mary Mills is this girl who was in the gifted school senior class. She played classical piano and had the prettiest hands I've ever seen. Even writing about her now makes me feel like my head is too heavy for my shoulders. She always had this look on her face like she was thinking about someplace far, far away. Like she was meant to live in a better, more primitive world where people walk around in loincloths and make their own tools or whatever. I just realized that I am writing about her in the past tense even though I'm sure she's still very much alive.

Mrs. Leene says I should think about people in the present tense.

"It forces you to take responsibility for them," she says.

I don't fully understand that concept, but I'll switch tenses anyway.

So Mary Mills's hair is beautifully black the way horses are black, and her eyes are as gray as the Michigan winter sky. Sometimes they change and look green. Once she was wearing this navy blue turtleneck sweater and her eyes looked *silver*. Like *jewelry* or something.

At the beginning of my junior year at the gifted school, there was a rumor floating around that Mary Mills was going to go to this elite conservatory in New York City called the Juilliard School, where apparently only a handful of our nation's most promising musicians, actors, and dancers are admitted. She performed at a school assembly once. Debussy, it was, I think. She played in front of the whole school for like an hour. This one piece called *Claire de Lune* haunted me for a long time.

I tried talking to her once, but she gave me the evil eye because I accidentally touched her. I didn't mean to, I swear—my hand just sort of reached out. She shot me this penetrating look, then I sort of bowed my head.

"Sorry about that," I offered.

My face was totally hot with shame.

27

For some reason, she sort of bowed her head, too, like we were about to do karate or something. I still can't figure out why she did that. When she looked up, her eyes were so gray-green pretty, I practically asked her to marry me right there at the Dr. Gordon Berlin Memorial Water Fountain.

I must confess that I do this thing sometimes where I close my eyes and envision Mary Mills playing the piano. She is sitting on the bench, facing away from the keys, and her breasts are just sort of floating out in front of her. Then she turns and starts to play and the music is really sad, sadder than *Claire de Lune,* sadder than old skinny trees in winter. And then I move toward her and everything slows down. Like slower than slow motion. And she might be crying a little and then I start comforting her and we're hugging and laughing a little and maybe I've got a stick of gum and I offer it to her and she says, "No thank you," but her mouth opens just enough so that I can see that she wants me to maybe kiss her, just enough for a penny to slip through, and she kind of flips her black hair over her shoulder and one thing leads to another and we start making love right there on the piano bench.

Jesus, that's a lot to take in.

Sorry.

I almost can't stand those thoughts, and yet again they're the ones that keep you going, right?

To be honest, there are only a few halfway decent-looking girls here at Burnstone Grove. That Silent Starla is pretty interesting. She has really milky-white skin, pale blue, dark-eyeliner eyes, and a nice smile, which she only exhibited once, after group when Dr. Shays asked if anyone ever prayed. We were talking about God and atheism and the subject of faith in general.

"Do any of you pray?" he asked.

Nobody answered. We just sort of looked around at each other.

"Starla?" he said.

"What?" she answered.

"Do you pray?"

"What?" she said again.

"Do you pray?" he stated very sternly, repeating himself.

"Like to God?" Starla asked.

"Yes," Dr. Shays answered.

That's when Starla started laughing in this very high-pitched tone. No one else laughed, and it made for an uncomfortable end of group. One of her teeth is gray, like it died or somehow got permanently stained. This characteristic makes her more interesting-looking— there's something about having a minor flaw like that.

I think Shannon Lynch has sort of a crush on her, so I won't meddle.

"She's sound," he says sometimes.

I don't know what that means. I think it's supposed to be British for sexy or something.

4

Last night this Blue Grouper named Gary Ship tried to hang himself with an extension cord. Apparently the thing snapped because it couldn't sustain his weight. One of the meds nurses found him sprawled under the fake Christmas tree in the lounge. He'd somehow secured the makeshift noose to a hook that holds the big dome light in the lounge. When the extension cord snapped, he sort of pitched into the Christmas tree. Now the tree is crooked and looks more turquoise than evergreen.

This morning at our session, the first thing Mrs. Leene asked me was if I was okay.

"Are you okay, Steve?" she asked. She was putting lotion on her hands and it was making the whole room smell good.

"I'm fine," I said. And I thought I was, until my hands started shaking like crazy. I guess I can't deny that the whole Gary Ship thing freaked me out a little. Part of me just wishes that anyone who wants to hang himself would just use a rope like you're supposed to. Welton with the necktie and Gary Ship with the extension cord. I mean, unless I'm missing something, there's not like some global shortage of rope.

Gary Ship found the extension cord in the lounge, where they were putting up the Christmas tree lights. You would think the Burnstone Grove administration would be more careful about stuff like that.

Gary Ship has a face like a koala bear, and Shannon told me that he earned a trip to Burnstone Grove three months ago because he was found half-dead in a refrigerated bin in the frozen-foods section of a Kroger's in Auburn Hills. He worked the graveyard shift cleaning supermarket floors with one of those oscillating buffers. He had attempted to slash his wrists with an ice scraper, of all things. I can just imagine the blood all over the Ben & Jerry's ice cream.

This morning they helicoptered him away to some hospital in Traverse City.

"We don't have to talk about Gary," Mrs. Leene said.

So we didn't.

I basically just sat there in her office and stared at the spines of her books. Which is okay with Mrs. Leene—she doesn't mind long silences. She says that sometimes the best thing to say is nothing at all and that just thinking with her can be useful, too.

So I've been thinking a lot about how my brother made me participate in his drug habit, and it sort of pisses me off. I thought nothing of it at the time, but looking back on it, I must admit that I possess a fair amount of anger toward him.

So this is what would usually happen.

When Welton got home from the nursing home, he would slide an envelope of pills under my bedroom door. Before the pills, it was a five-dollar bill, which was to be used to purchase his daily bottle of Robitussin at the Piggly Wiggly. He'd always let me keep the change. I'm still not sure if that was out of generosity or if he just forgot there was money coming back to him.

After a few months, the cough medicine money was replaced by a small manila envelope of pills with *Bury in the backyard. Thanks, bro.* written on the front.

I kept the pills in a Mason jar that Welton put on my dresser. It had THE ITTY-BITTY PHARMACY written in black permanent marker on the front. It wasn't important to Welton that I separate or organize the pills in any special way. Some were small and colorful. Others were these big white pharmaceutical hockey pucks. I think he took them as arbitrarily as I put them in the jar.

"What are these, anyway?" I asked him once.

"Just pills," he said.

"What kind of pills?" I asked.

"The kind that make you feel stuff."

Once I took one. It was of the larger, blondish, UFO-shaped variety, and it made me sad and lethargic. I kept thinking about the sycamore tree in our front yard and how it smelled like graphite pencils and how I used to climb it and how I saw my dad urinate on it once. It was just after my mom got diagnosed and she was having trouble using the toilet and he couldn't hold his bladder. He was too much of a coward to go in the sink like Welton and me. He would rather urinate on a tree, right there in the front yard for all the neighbors and the rest of the world to see.

After I took the pill, I slept for like twelve hours and woke up in the early afternoon. Welton called the gifted school pretending to be my dad. He could do voices pretty well. He was especially good at my dad, but he could also imitate Homer Simpson and the guy who does the monster truck commercials on the radio.

Welton told the secretary at the gifted school that I got food poisoning and that there was a chance that I would have to miss the following day, too. That was probably the coolest thing he ever did for me. . . .

It's like ten at night right now, and Shannon just came into my room and told me that Gary Ship died in the helicopter on his way to that hospital in Traverse City. There's supposed to be some sort of memorial service tomorrow night after dinner.

I just have to say that I'm so sick of people dying wherever I go.

5

So last night that memorial service for Gary Ship was unbelievably stupid.

The faculty all took turns sharing their various illuminating thoughts. This heavyset woman with this gross curlicue chin hair whom I've never seen before (apparently she's the chairwoman of the Burnstone Grove board) talked about community healing and how grief is simply a kind of weather system and how we can all be shelter for each other until this "unfortunate" weather passes. She took her glasses off and put them back on about fifty times, as if her thoughts were too expansive for her own head. Dr. Shays spoke about choices and the concept that what makes us different from animals is that we have the ability to choose and that Gary Ship made a very conscious choice to "harm himself." I have no idea what his point was. I mean, of course he made a choice to harm himself with that extension cord! It wasn't like the thing wrapped itself around his neck and strung him up while he was sleeping!

Mrs. Leene was the only one who said anything that halfway made sense, which was about how in some way maybe it was *good* that Gary Ship finally got to leave us because he was in such pain about stuff. That's all she said and then she sat back down. She got a few funny looks from her Burnstone Grove cohorts or whatever they're called, but she wouldn't look back at them. She had tears in her eyes, too, which I thought was sort of nice.

Later the Blue Groupers went into the TV lounge and played this Nick Drake album called "Five Leaves Left." I guess Nick Drake was this English singer-songwriter guy who committed suicide in his mom's house when he was like twenty-seven. His stuff sounded pretty sad and folky. Shannon says that his suicide is a bit of a mystery—that no one could officially discern whether he took too much sleeping medication intentionally or not—but that as far as singer-songwriters go, he was ahead of his time.

I thought it was cool how the Blue Groupers gathered together in private like that.

If something like that happened to me, I would appreciate that kind of gathering.

So back to bibliotherapy. . . .

When thinking back on stuff, especially things that happened toward the end of last summer, I find that the notion of time gets weird for me.

Events jump out of order, and sometimes I can't place the stuff with my mom and the stuff with Welton. It gets all jumbled in my head, so please bear with me. I'll do my best.

I think things started going bad that day at Greyhound Park. Just before the bridge to Foote, there's this dog track. There are fourteen races a day—twenty-eight on Saturdays—and entire like *sects* of senior citizens from Chicago and Milwaukee and Madison come over by the busload to spend the afternoon eating five-dollar hot dogs and blowing their Social Security checks on the pheromonal whims of half-starved, fleet-footed dogs.

I like to go because I'm pretty good at handicapping my bets. I can usually score on a quinella or two, and if I don't get killed early, I can walk away having made twenty or thirty bucks. Success at the dog track is all pretty random. Once I lost two hundred on the last four races after I'd pocketed three-fifty on the first ten.

So it was a Saturday in July, a week or so after the fireworks over the river had given enough of a cheap thrill to get the local Feet (that's what I call the citizens of Foote) through the rest of the summer, and I decided to go to the dog track.

When I think about it now, I'm sure part of going there had to do with my mom—she was pretty far along in hospice care then, and nobody knew how many days she had left. I mean, I wasn't constantly thinking about her or anything like that. Maybe I was just going through this phase where I didn't feel like being *anywhere, ever,* and the dog track was about the best alternative to falling down a mineshaft or something like that.

At the Piggly Wiggly, I wrote a check to cash for a hundred bucks and headed west toward the river.

Our house is about a fifteen-minute walk from the track. I have to say that walking through East Foote isn't particularly exciting. The houses look like they're made out of stale gingerbread, and all the parked cars seem sad and dirty and half broken-down.

I don't recall the exact temperature that day, but it was so hot that little neighborhood kids were running through sprinkler systems in their underwear. Their slow, overweight mothers were sitting next to bird feeders and ceramic deer and blue plastic pools, shoving cold cuts and Fig Newtons and macaroni salad into their mouths, while strange, sexless men (their husbands) trimmed the hedges and pulled up dandelions, their wet, hairless legs all white and rubbery-looking. I don't mean to be gross, but that's really what my neighborhood is like.

As I approached the highway, I was suddenly

downwind of the river. The Mississippi smelled pretty bad that day—like sewage and catfish and rotten crawdads festering in the same thick stew. You eventually get used to it, but late in the summer, when it gets warm and humid, it takes a few weeks to adjust to the general rot of things.

You're supposed to be eighteen to get into Greyhound Park, but they never card me, because I'm tall and when I want to, I can give off a fair amount of sophisticated energy. I've found that it's all about the way you walk and the way you reveal your money. Just slow down and let the bills grace your fingertips like they're a nice handkerchief or something. The guy in the little turnstile hut loves it when you're nonchalant with your money.

Despite the heat and the smell of the river, it was a perfect July day. The sky was so blue, it almost looked fake. I was wearing a pair of jeans and my blue Explosions in the Sky T-shirt. Explosions in the Sky is this band from Austin. They record these amazing ten-minute songs with no lyrics. They're totally anti-radio, way above it in my opinion. Welton turned me on to them after he came back from one of their shows in Madison.

I'd missed the first six races, and as I was passing through the gates, I could see that they were showing the dogs for the seventh. The grandstand was about half-full, and everyone was smoking and drinking enormous plastic cups of beer. I was starving, so I got an order of nachos and pop and made my way to the rail so I could study the dogs.

I was immediately drawn to the eight dog. It had these totally muscular forelegs, and ten pounds on the seven dog. I always go with a heavy eight dog if they have good times, because they can take the hits around the first turn. Despite the eight dog's previous two finishes (a win and a show), the odds were 32–1. It was a few minutes before post time. I weaved my way through the crowd and put twenty dollars on the eight dog to win, ten on it to place, and ten to show—forty dollars total, which is pretty risky for a first bet.

After I got my tickets, I went down to the front to watch the race. I like to get as close to the rail as possible, because sometimes when the greyhounds pass, you can totally feel the wind breaking off of them.

I grabbed the rail and waited for the bone pole. I always grab the rail when the bone pole starts its slow, screeching arc toward the box. It's a weird little ritual, I admit, but I do it for good luck, and you have to deal with superstition when you're betting on dogs. I remember that the only thought in my head was that I was feeling pretty good. Not great or anything. Just good. The sun was on my face and the nachos tasted pretty good and they put just the right amount of crushed ice in my pop, the way I like it.

Then the bell rang and the kennels flew open and the shouts boiled up from the grandstand. I looked at the board and saw that the odds on the eight dog had dropped to 24–1. Despite the last-minute plummet, it was still possible to make some decent money. I would buy this car I'd seen for sale that morning in our neighbor's driveway. It was a midnight blue Caprice Classic with only thirty thousand miles on it—new tires and everything—and they were selling it for four hundred dollars. I would road-trip to Vermont or Canada and just like hike around for a few weeks before school started up.

About halfway through the race, I realized that my eight dog was boxed in the middle and unless a miracle happened, he wouldn't be able to break out of it.

On the backstretch my eight dog finally got free and came up around the outside. The grandstand was going crazy, and for the briefest moment I thought I would get my miracle. But the four dog won by five lengths and my eight dog finished sixth. But even though I had lost my first race, I took my eight dog's late surge as a promising sign. I pictured that Caprice Classic in my neighbor's yard and counted my money.

The dogs for the eighth were being chaperoned to the front for their showings. I was particularly impressed with the four dog. It had had four top-two finishes in a row and had a nice inside position.

I made my way to the betting counter and put a twelve-dollar wheel on the four dog. The nice thing about a quinella wheel is that to win, all your dog has to do is finish in the top two. Obviously it's nice if it finishes with a high-odds dog, because the payoff's better.

Near the betting counter, I heard this old guy who I always saw at the track telling someone about the five dog and how it was a sleeper, how in a practice race down in Waterloo, it dead-heated with one of the top dogs on the circuit. I had an impulse to change my bet and go with the five dog, but I second-guessed it and stayed with my pick.

The dogs had been boxed, and the bone pole was making its slow sweep around the track.

When the kennels flew open, my stomach knotted up and I was so excited I could hardly breathe.

When I looked up, the four dog was in third place, a half a length off the lead. People were clinging to the fence and the cheers from the grandstand started swelling again.

Then out of nowhere, the one dog raced toward the lead. It was a dead heat for the last fifty yards. At the finish there were the kind of cheers you hear at monster truck shows.

It was a photo finish. My four dog was mixed in with the five dog and the surging one dog. I was positioned too far to the left of the line to make a guess. To the naked eye it appeared that my four dog was easily among the top two, but photo results are always so loaded with politics and larceny, you'd need a busload of nuns and half the National Guard to obtain an outcome with any kind of moral decency.

Suddenly more shouts rose up and the results were posted on the board. The one dog had finished first, sharing the quinella with the five dog, which had 83–1 odds to win. If I'd gone with the five dog, I'd have won $537.

I have to admit that I was tempted to bet again. That's what happens when you lose a tight one like that—you get bitter and you start getting reckless. I only had ten bucks left, and I decided not to blow the rest of it on the ninth. Instead I went and sat in the grandstand for the rest of the day. I didn't bet on another race, but I picked three winners. All two dogs, strangely enough.

By the fourteenth race, the place had pretty much cleared out except for the desperate ones who were still hoping to reverse all their bad luck. I clung to my ten bucks and just watched.

At the end of the day, some old lady with a stuffed Velcro monkey clinging to her straw hat screamed and nearly fainted because she'd won fourteen hundred dollars on the superfecta. A security guard had to help her to the counter to collect.

Good for her, I thought. *Maybe she'll buy herself a new hat.*

I crossed the highway just before dusk.

I'd like to believe that if I'd played that five dog, everything would be different now. I would have easily bought our neighbor's Caprice Classic and taken that road trip and hiked or camped in Vermont or Canada or wherever, and I know it's stupid, but part of me wants to believe that maybe my mom wouldn't have died and Welton wouldn't have hanged himself with that necktie. I know it's absurd to think those things, I really do, but I can't help it. The smallest victory can affect a lot of things.

Enormous trucks filled with beef and coffee beans and office furniture screamed by on the highway. I had this thought that if one of them hit you, you wouldn't even feel it. It would be like turning off the light.

6

So that night after the races, I crossed the bridge and walked home through the hot, mosquito-infested neighborhoods of East Foote.

I walked past the Amoco station and the ice-cream shop and the parking lot of the Piggly Wiggly, where kids on skateboards were trying to imitate stunts they'd seen on MTV.

When I came through the front door, my dad was asleep in his living-room chair. The TV light was making his face look somehow pained. I could hear one of the hospice nurses talking to my mom in her room. They were discussing the new orthopedic toilet seat they'd just installed in the bathroom. It was like two feet thick and made it easier for my mom to sit, because she had been having a lot of trouble with her hips. That thing made me so nervous, I stopped using the bathroom altogether. I must have urinated in the sink a hundred times that week.

I went into the kitchen and rooted around in the cupboards for a few minutes. The only thing that seemed the least bit edible was a bag of Chex Party Mix, so I grabbed that and went back to my room. I sat down at my desk and went sort of blank for a while. After eating a few handfuls of the Chex Party Mix, I took a pack of Camel Lights out from the top drawer of my desk. I'd only been smoking for a few weeks, and I wasn't very good at it yet. I don't even know why I started the stupid habit, if you want to know the truth. I guess I had to do *something* to keep boredom at bay. The house was starting to smell all damp and sickly, and smoking killed the stench a bit.

I had no plans that evening and I was sort of depressed from blowing most of my money at the dog track, so I decided I would just go to bed early and sleep for like sixteen hours. So I took my shoes off and I was about to get ready for bed when I heard my mom call for me. Whenever she would call out my name like that—especially during her last few weeks—it was like getting thumped between the shoulder blades with a hammer.

In the hospice room, my mom was trying to reach the straw from her water cup. She was totally bald at this point, and the whites of her eyes had dulled to this weird brownish gray. She only weighed eighty-something pounds and her lips had sort of disappeared. My mouth hurts just imagining her.

"Steven," she said, "help me drink, honey."

The hospice nurse had been using this citrus-smelling disinfectant, but her room still stank pretty bad. There was a yellow stool in her bedpan and the sight of it almost made me retch.

"Come here," my mom said.

I took a step toward her and I could see a new growth pressing through her forehead. There were things emerging all over her lately. At first they were calling it breast cancer, but now it was everywhere. A few weeks before, the oncologist had discovered a tumor in her abdomen that was the size of a baseball.

I tried not to focus on her forehead and stepped closer. When I reached for the water cup I practically knocked her morphine cartridge out of her arm. It beeped a few times, but I steadied it and helped her drink. Her breath smelled like eggs and pepper.

"Where's your father?" she asked after she finished drinking. Her voice sounded like it had been cut in half.

"He's in the living room watching TV," I said.

"Did he shave today?"

I said, "I don't know."

"Ask him to shave, will you, Steven?"

"Sure," I said.

One of her tubes looked clogged. It made me feel like I couldn't breathe.

"Where's Welton?" she asked.

"I don't know," I answered. "I think he's over in Foote."

She coughed, and went, "Tell him I had a dream about him. Will you do that for me?"

"I'll tell him."

"We were at the circus and his pants kept falling down. It was funny. Tell him that for me, okay, honey?"

I said, "Sure, Mom."

After that, she took my hand and asked me to do an Our Father with her. I knelt down at the side of her bed and bowed my head. She took my hands with one of hers, and we began. Her fingers were bloated and soft. While we prayed, I sort of went blank. I kept waiting for something to stir inside—like a holy fluttering or whatever—but it never came. I could hear my own voice praying, and I hated how high it was.

When we were through praying, my mom fell asleep. She might have even drifted off during the part about the Kingdom and the Power and the Glory. I took my hands back and watched her for a minute.

Even though her mouth was all dried and shriveled, she was sort of smiling. The morphine always made her happy. I must confess here that there was a time or two when I was tempted to slip the needle into my own vein just to see what it was like, but that would have been heinous.

There was a breeze coming though her window, and the moonlight made her teeth look sort of gray.

I slid my hands out from under hers and quietly left her room.

In the living room, my dad was still in his La-Z-Boy. He was asleep and the TV was still on, with the sound turned down. It was some old black-and-white movie, and these two gangster types in expensive raincoats were shaking hands on the deck of a ship. One looked like he wanted to kill the other one. My dad's mouth was open and there was a snore caught in his throat. He somehow looked like he was dying of thirst.

I nudged his shoulder a couple of times and he stirred and then his eyes opened. The whites were pink and dull-looking.

"Steven," he said. "Everything okay?" His voice was small and congested.

"Mom wants you to shave," I said.

It's weird. He was staring at me like he was feeling

guilty about something. It seemed almost like he wanted me to punish him or something. There were long, gray whiskers all over his face.

After a minute he nodded, touching his face.

"So are you gonna shave?" I asked for some reason.

"Yeah," he said. "I'll shave tonight. Before I go to bed."

But I knew that was a lie because he would never even make it to his room. He would fall asleep in the La-Z-Boy like he had every night for the past week and a half.

When I got back to my room, I wasn't tired anymore. I was completely agitated, if you want to know the truth. I really have no idea why. Maybe it was because of the way my dad was just sitting there in the living room all slothful and dehydrated.

There's this picture of Jesus that I have over my desk. My mom put it there when I was a little kid. She used to make me pray to him before I went to bed. Jesus looks completely malnourished and sort of sad and hopeful at the same time. I had this weird urge to X out his eyes. I even opened the top drawer to my desk and grabbed a black permanent marker—I removed the cap and everything—but when it came down to it, I couldn't do it—it was like there was this force field around Jesus or something—so I put the cap back on and dropped it on my desk.

All of a sudden, for some reason, my room felt like it was shrinking, like the walls were totally closing in on me.

So that's when I left.

The keys to the Fairmont were on the kitchen table. I grabbed them and stuffed them into my pocket. I figured no one else would be using them anytime soon.

7

So I headed east on Highway 20.

Even though I never usually wear one, I put my seat belt on because the minute I pulled out of the driveway, I started having these totally gothic visions of my own brains being splattered on the inside of the windshield.

Healthy, right?

After about ten miles, Highway 20 turns into a two-lane snail stream dominated by semis. Passing is essential if you want to get anywhere fast.

Even though it wasn't ten o'clock yet, it seemed like that kind of late when you can hear the secrets hidden in the droning of crickets and power lines and that slow, creepy leaning of corn. It's probably because of how with regard to the modern world, the places around Foote and East Foote are still like forty years behind. Most of them don't even have fast-food restaurants, and the majority of them are called townships.

The highway was dark, and every time a car came toward me, I kept thinking it was a cop. I mean I had my license and all that—I wasn't technically doing anything illegal. I guess I felt like I was sort of on the run or something, and when I think about it now, maybe I was.

I turned the radio on to this talk show. Some totally paranoid evangelist-slash-DJ was riffing about gangs in Los Angeles and how many weapons the Crips and the Bloods have been stockpiling over the years. According to the host, the West Coast gangs had enough artillery to take over the state of California.

A bunch of loners started calling in and giving their opinions. One woman from Omaha, Nebraska, said she'd seen a movie about a gang but that they weren't mean at all. She said that they were actually very talented singers and dancers and that for them it had nothing to do with guns or drugs. For them, she said, it was all about the ownership of certain New York City rooftops.

Another caller said that perhaps it was simply a sign of the times that a mongrel people was organizing and perfecting its systems of violence. Then he admitted to owning a few weapons himself. The redneck was so drunk you could practically smell the fumes coming through the speakers.

I got bored with the radio after about fifteen minutes and turned it off. The last thing I needed was more insanity in my life.

I had just passed Galena, Illinois, and was a few miles from Elizabeth, which is this little Hallmark card that boasts about four houses. I had no idea where I was actually going, except that it was east. For a second I entertained the idea of heading all the way to Chicago.

I imagined myself standing on the shores of Lake Michigan, the city totally like throbbing behind me, my hair blowing like crazy.

Suddenly the steering wheel was vibrating. For a second I thought that something had broken—an axle or the steering column or whatever—but then I realized it was me. I looked at my hands and they were trembling so bad I thought the veins in my wrists would burst.

A semi passed, and when its headlights filled the Fairmont, it made me focus on the road again. When I looked at the speedometer, I realized that I was going almost eighty miles an hour, which meant that the semi was going at least ninety. It was definitely the fastest I have ever driven, and I'm lucky I didn't crash.

That's when I started doing the Our Father again. I have no idea why. It just sort of poured out of me. And I recited it way too fast, like there was some sort of creepy priest in the back seat trying to damn me or something. But when I got to the part about the Kingdom, the Power, and the Glory, I said the Kingdom, the Power, and the *Gory*. I even repeated the line, knowing that I was making a mistake, but *Gory* just kept coming out. It felt like someone else was making me say it, which is a pretty frightening situation when you're all alone and you've just hijacked your parents' car.

When I got to Elizabeth, I pulled over to a Shell station and I got full service. I was sort of hyperventilating, so I had to take a moment to catch my breath.

Behind the gas station there was this huge cornfield that was so vast and unending it somehow looked like if you walked into it, you would disappear forever. The stalks were probably six feet tall. It was a starless night. The moon was low and huge and yellow, and it somehow made everything look blue. And the breeze was all strange and eerie. It was almost like the field was breathing.

I killed the engine and asked the gas-station attendant guy to fill it up with regular. He was like fifty years old, a veteran tobacco-chewer with old-man strength.

While he was washing the windshield, he was sort of staring at me through the glass. He spit some tobacco juice off to the side and kept washing without missing a beat. You have to wonder how a guy like that winds up working at a gas station in the middle of nowhere. For some reason he was really starting to make me nervous—maybe it was because of how he hadn't yet uttered a single word. I slid out of the car and headed toward the station. Behind me I could hear the squeegee sort of crying on the windshield, but I didn't dare look back because I was afraid he would still be staring at me.

Inside the gas station, I bought a Coke and headed back to the car. I paid the attendant guy and stood staring at the cornfield for a minute.

"You okay, son?" the gas-station attendant asked. He had a deep, sleepy voice.

"I'm okay," I said.

He waited till I got in, and then he shut the door for me. He was a lot nicer than I thought he would be.

"Drive safe, now," he said, and then headed back into the gas station.

I sat there for a moment and thought about my mom. It was her groans of pain that would get me the most. Sometimes they didn't even sound human. Sometimes she sounded like a cow, and for some weird reason, that made me think about hamburgers and I suddenly realized how starved I was.

I started the car and headed back toward the highway.

8

Well, I think it's pretty obvious that I never made it to Chicago.

I never even made it past Elizabeth, Illinois, if you want to know the truth.

In fact, when I left that Shell station, I turned right around on Highway 20 and headed back to East Foote.

By the time I got home, it was maybe 11:30 P.M., but I couldn't say for sure. I was shocked to discover that my dad had actually gotten himself off the La-Z-Boy and gone upstairs to bed. The house felt weirdly deserted. It was so quiet, you could hear the clock in the kitchen.

I seriously was going to make hamburgers, but there was no ground beef. All I could find were a couple of steaks in the freezer, but they would have taken hours to thaw, so I microwaved some Chunky beef stew and drank about half a gallon of milk.

I felt sick and depressed after that.

So depressed that I decided to call Mary Mills.

During the summer she would practice the piano at the gifted school. The building was supposed to be closed, but she had some special privilege because of her big Juilliard audition. Toward the end of June, I would crawl in through a tornado panel in the chemistry lab and take my shoes off and sneak down the hall and watch her through the window in the door to the recital hall. I know that that's a bit stalker-like, me spying on her like that, but I never meant any harm. I just really liked to hear her play.

So the painful truth is that Mary used to date this totally thick-necked, silent guy named Shane O'Meara. He went to Carroll High School—the big, prestigious parochial school in Foote—and he was the star of the football team and shaved his head and he was this totally devoted Catholic, too, like he wouldn't have premarital sex or anything and there was this rumor that he was going to play linebacker for the University of Wisconsin in the Big Ten. Instead of going to Madison, he decided to stay home and play at Governors College in Foote. His choice to stay home and play at the smaller school made him a local hero. He was written up in the *Foote Bugle* like nine times that year.

Some people said O'Meara stayed because of Mary Mills, but they broke up at some point during the first semester. Rumor has it that she got pregnant and they got an abortion down in Iowa City. Who knows if that's true, though? Rumors are like roaches. All I know is that she used to wear this totally sacred ring he gave her—some Irish love band or whatever—and one day she came to school and she wasn't wearing it anymore.

So I mustered some courage and grabbed the Foote phone book. I stared at it for about twelve minutes, and then I leafed through and found the *M*'s. I called all seventeen listings under *Mills*—at least half of them hung up on me—till I got Mary's house. This totally bored, monotone guy answered. I think he was her father. He sounded like he was either pissed off or drunk, like some alcoholic country-and-western singer or whatever. I imagined him wearing spurs and a lot of turquoise. He called for Mary and she picked up another phone.

"Hello?"

Her voice was like something impossible that you long for. Like the ability to fly or breathe water.

I was like, "Hey, Mary."

"Who is this?" she asked.

"It's Steve," I replied.

She said, "Steve *who*?"

"Steve from the gifted school. Steve Nugent."

"*White* Steve *the Mathlete?*"

"Yeah," I said. "White Steve the Mathlete."

Man, to be known as White Steve the Mathlete is pretty embarrassing. But it's true—I was a Mathlete. I was ranked second on the team, in fact, and fourth in the whole Mississippi Valley Conference.

There was a pause.

I could hear her swallowing.

"What do you want?" she asked.

"Um," I said, "I don't want anything."

"Oh," she said.

Things were obviously going nowhere fast.

"How are you?" I asked.

There was another pause. I heard a TV in the background. It sounded like some kind of Western. Cowboys were fighting with Indians, and horses were galloping across the dusty desert plains or whatever.

"Why are you calling me?" Mary then asked. She didn't say it mean or anything—she just asked it.

I took a deep breath and said, "I don't know. I just wanted to say hey."

"Oh," she said. "Hey."

"Hey," I stupidly said back.

"It's going on midnight, Steve," she noted.

"Yeah, sorry about that," I offered.

"How'd you get my number?"

"Um," I said. "From like the phone book."

This was definitely turning out to be a mistake. I said, "I guess I sort of needed to ask you something."

"What?"

I thought I was going to ask her if she wanted to maybe get together—to like go bowling or see a movie or something—but that's not even close to what came out.

Instead I said, "Do you think George Washington really chopped down that cherry tree?"

"What?" she said, obviously a bit thrown. I don't blame her—I would've been thrown too. But I couldn't quite seem to make any sense. Maybe it was because I kept picturing her standing there in her nightgown. Her dewy shoulders aglow in her kitchen and all that.

"George Washingmachine," I remember hearing myself saying. "Do you think that cherry tree thing even *happened*?"

I have no idea why these particular words were coming out of my mouth. I mean, I hadn't been thinking about George Washington at all. And the fact that I said *Washingmachine*—how crazy is that? The strange thing, though, was that I really wanted her opinion on the matter, and I wanted it so bad that it almost started to feel like I was involved in a life-or-death situation. I was so nervous, I think my teeth were chattering.

"Steve, I have to go," Mary said.

"I mean, you can totally *tell* he was lying about not being able to tell a lie," I continued. "Just look at him on the nickel."

"I have to go to *bed*."

"Wait," I begged.

"I really have to go, Steve. Bye."

"I love you!" I cried.

She was like, "You *what*?"

It was too late. I couldn't take it back.

"I love you," I repeated.

"Oh," she said. "You do?"

"Yes," I answered.

Then things went blank. I could have been a fish in an aquarium. Just floating there without a brain.

On the other end, that Western was reaching new limits of Indian war cries. It sounded like they were finally going to win one for a change.

I started to open my mouth, but nothing would come out. Neither of us spoke. For a second I thought maybe she dropped the phone.

Then I heard her dad's voice in the background.

He said, "Bed, Mare."

He sounded totally dead. Like he was one of those bodies with a voice. No heart and no blood. Not even a lung. Just a body and a voice.

"You play so beautifully, Mary," I said. "You're better than Beethoven and all those guys. You're so much better —"

That's when she hung up.

I was so in love, I went into my room and drank half a bottle of Robitussin. It was maximum strength for cough and cold. I decided to change my clothes and put on this gabardine cowboy shirt that Welton let me borrow last Halloween. It has black deerskin shoulders, red sleeves, pearl snaps, and blond tubing. He bought it in Barcelona during this European trip he took with his underclassmen AAU basketball team, just after his sophomore year. I never gave it back, but he didn't care. He stopped changing his clothes after he lost his job at the nursing home. Or maybe it was even before that. He would like totally lounge around in these old brown suit slacks my mom used to make him wear to church. The brown suit slacks and his green orderly top from the nursing home. It was an odd combination. It made him look like he was either just being admitted or released from the hospital.

Anyway, I changed into Welton's gabardine cowboy shirt, and even though it was still like eighty-five degrees, I put on a pair of brown corduroy pants and I started sort of dancing around the room. Nothing too fast. Just a little two-step. And Mary Mills was like right there with me. Obviously she wasn't really there, but I sort of pretended like she was the bottle of Robitussin and I was dancing with her and drinking her sweet delicious tears.

And then all of a sudden I realized how little time we have. Like on the earth, I mean. And when I say *we,* I mean everyone. It was a profound realization, and I suddenly had to share this fact with Mary. I know that sounds insane because of how it was already after midnight and all the other crazy things that had happened that day, but it was one of the most important feelings I've ever had—my chest was swelling and everything.

It felt like there were only so many hours left on the earth—that's the hardest part about being alive.

Mary Mills would be going off to New York City in a few weeks and there was just too little time!

That's when I decided to rehijack the Fairmont. Before I left, I brushed my teeth and reapplied Old Spice High Endurance deodorant stick. I put on this after-shave that my dad keeps in the bathroom, too. It's green and it's the kind you use for an electric razor. It has a masculine smell and I'm pretty sure girls like it.

9

So before I continue, I have to tell you about this dream I had last night, which was the night after the Gary Ship memorial service.

The dream went like this:

I was a stainless-steel robot. I had been put together with circuits and switches. When I opened my mouth to speak, a sound like the highway came out. Like a convoy of semis blaring under viaducts on Interstate 90. It was dark and I was alone until I walked through this huge silver gate. I passed through the gate and happened upon this secret graveyard, where I saw this huge like Lollapalooza gathering of other robots. There were thousands of them. We all pretty much looked the same, which is perhaps best described by the term "factory-built." The graves were already dug. Each robot had its own plot. Mine had all of these pink flowers around the rim. They were the pinkest flowers I've ever seen. I'm pretty sure they were tulips. I joined the other robots and we formed these huge militaristic platoons of doom, and then one by one we stepped down into our graves. We weren't instructed to do it—no one gave us orders or anything—we just somehow knew what we were supposed to do, like it was our *fate*.

But when it came to my turn, I couldn't go through with it. The other robots were screaming at me—there was so much highway noise I thought my robot head would pop off—but I wouldn't budge. Instead, I started eating all the tulips. One by one at first and then by the armful.

When I woke up, my mouth tasted like a Nerf ball and I was covered in a cold sweat. I lurched toward my trusty Burnstone Grove sink and pounded about four cups of water. Man, I couldn't stop panting.

I felt so lost and alone that I wound up curling into a ball on the other bed and sort of freezing like that. I don't know why I chose the other bed. Maybe I felt somehow betrayed by mine, that it wasn't like *protecting* me or something. It took me a while to fall back asleep, and I tried to distract my terrible thoughts of loneliness and insomnia by listening to the Burnstone Grove pipes knocking. At night the whole facility constantly belches like it's suffering from architectural indigestion or something.

I was particularly humiliated in the morning when I woke to discover that I had urinated the bed.

"What do you think the dream means?" Mrs. Leene asked at our session today.

"I don't know," I said. "Maybe that I'm afraid of graves."

"Hmmm," she said. "I think there's more to it than just that."

But as usual she didn't push.

I didn't tell her about how I urinated in the bed of my future, still-undisclosed roommate. I told the old Mexican maintenance guy about it, though, and he was cool.

"Some guys came in here and did that in the middle of the night," I lied. He just nodded and told me he'd take care of it.

"I take care," he said.

Later I came back from lunch and he had replaced the mattress and everything.

The other thing Mrs. Leene brought up today was the subject of lithium, which is this psychoactive drug they give you if you're what they call bipolar or manic-depressive. Lithium somehow keeps you from emotionally peaking too high or dropping too low.

"It evens you out," Mrs. Leene explained.

I imagined myself walking around in a leisure suit listening to elevator music or something.

"I'm not sure you need it," she added. "The other

day it was brought up for discussion at our faculty meeting. I just wanted to let you know."

So I haven't slept much and I'm not sure how this is all coming out.

Lithium   lithium   lithium   lithium   lithium lithium . . .

But dinner's in less than forty-five minutes and they're serving potpies, which are my favorite, and I have to get back to this whole thing with Mary Mills.

So where was I?

Mary Mills lives in Foote over near Founders High School, where the houses are so upright and similar it's like the neighborhood was modeled after some weird science-fiction novel. Blond brick and manicured lawns and jumbo-size, calligraphy numbers on the garage doors. Chimneys and satellite dishes, too. And all those German cars parked in the driveways. Cars just sitting there like enormous sleeping beetles. The houses in that part of Foote are so big it's like they have their own thoughts. Like after the humans go to sleep, they engage in these totally weird telepathic conversations with each other.

While I was crossing the bridge to Foote, I saw squad-car lights in the rearview mirror. In the middle of the night there's nothing like a cop to make you feel paranoid. After the bridge, I slowed down so he could pass me. Fortunately it wasn't a cop after all—it was a tow truck pulling this huge Cadillac. What was weird was that there was a man sleeping in the front seat of the Caddy. His head was resting on the steering wheel, and for a second I couldn't tell if he was alive or dead.

I checked in the rearview mirror a few more times, but all I could see was my own face staring back. I had this crazy feeling that the me in the mirror would start chewing *gum* or something. And I didn't even *have* any gum. In fact, I hadn't chewed gum in months! I looked about five times, and I kept getting that creepy gum feeling, so I turned the mirror down.

For some reason, I decided to stop off at my dad's electronics shop. He had given me a set of keys the previous summer so I could go in on weekends and help him and Lyman Singer clean up the store. I hadn't been there in a long time, but I figured I could take a few minutes and get myself together.

Just after my mom started her chemo treatments, my dad spent most of his time going to flea markets to buy and trade things for the store. He would usually drive to Iowa City or Cedar Rapids and sometimes he'd road-trip all the way out to Council Bluffs for the smallest thing.

Once he got a call from a friend who saw a vintage Victrola record player at a garage sale in Dordt, which is all the way on the other side of the state. Sure enough, he gassed up the Fairmont and left that morning like he was going on some historical fishing trip or something. He forked out over two hundred bucks for the Victrola and spent the night in a Motel Six, and when he called home, he raved about the record player like it was the thing that was going to cure my mom's cancer.

When I keyed into the shop, I could see the Victrola still sitting on a shelf behind the register. It was marked down from $350 to $180. My dad wouldn't even make the money back that he'd spent for it. The first thing I did when I saw the price tag was mark it up to $400. I used this black Sharpie that was next to the cash register. I put an exclamation point after the price, too. And then I wrote OR ELSE! I don't even know what that was supposed to mean, but I wrote it and it made me feel more effective than I had all day.

After that, I started snooping around the shop. To be honest, I have no idea what I was looking for, but I have to admit that I was acting sort of desperate.

There were boom boxes and console office phones and old clock radios from the sixties. There were toaster ovens and electric toothbrushes. There were six-foot lamps and rotisserie hot-dog grills. There were chrome things and wooden things and things with dials that I couldn't name.

I walked into the back room, where they keep all the really prime vintage stuff that my dad and Lyman Singer found at garage sales and at this obscure flea market they used to go to up in Fond du Lac, Wisconsin. Then suddenly, just as I was about to put my hand on this old milk-shake machine from the fifties, all of these clocks chimed. There were grandfather clocks and these things that were sort of like half-grandfather clocks, and so many cuckoo clocks I suddenly felt like I was trapped in some weird pop-up book for little kids. It scared me so bad I just about had a stroke. That would have been pretty pathetic to die of a stroke at sixteen. Behind me there was this one particular cuckoo clock that looked about three thousand years old. This *thing* flew through the clock's doors, and before I even realized what had happened, my hand shot up and broke it off. When I opened my hand, I was holding this totally deformed, premature-looking half-chicken. It was maybe the evilest thing I'd ever seen in my life. For some reason I started kind of choking it. Now, I know that's almost like serial-killer nuts or whatever, and I'm not asking you to try to understand—I swear I'm not—but that's what I did. I choked the thing between my thumbs and forefingers as if my life depended on it. When it felt like it was good and dead, I dropped the thing on the floor and stepped on it. My heart was beating so fast, I put my hand on my chest, as if that would help it slow down.

It was one o'clock in the morning, and I had just murdered the little bird that pops out of a cuckoo clock. And I still had so much to tell Mary! But I couldn't go yet. I started looking at all the other things in the back room. It was loaded with TVs. I was wearing my steel-toed Red Wing construction boots, so I decided to finally find out how useful they really were. When I kicked in the first TV—a nineteen-inch Magnavox with wicker speaker panels—it felt like the most perfect thing I had done in a long time. And there's nothing like the feeling of perfection that will inspire repeated behavior. So what I did was I went from TV screen to TV screen and just started kicking away. None of them broke on the first kick. One caved in after three. The sound it made was better than birds. It was way better than waterfalls or wind chimes. I didn't even care that I had a bunch of glass falling in my boot.

When I was through, I counted the TVs. There's something about numbers in a moment like that. Maybe it's because they're good for lore. Someday I would tell my grandkids that I kicked in seventeen TVs at my dad's electronics shop. They'd be proud, right?

After gathering the necessary data, I turned and sort of limped out. My shin was totally burning, but I had to lock up and get over to Mary's house before it was too late. According to all those clocks, when I left, it was almost two in the morning.

When I finally got to Mary's house, I parked about four blocks away, because I knew walking would help with the head-spinning sensation I was having, and I'm glad I did, because I had to stop against a tree and vomit. It was mostly that beef stew and the milk, but I won't go into too much detail—don't worry. I felt better almost immediately, although I must admit I was a little guilt-ridden about puking on somebody's tree.

Mary's house was blond brick, like the others. I sort of walked around their property a couple of times just to scope things out.

The backyard was full of that strange, hypnotic buzz of crickets. From the patio I could see into the kitchen. I pressed my face up against the sliding doors and watched my breath fog on the glass for a second. Someone had left a light on over the stove. They had this huge white refrigerator that looked like you could store five years' worth of food in it. The countertops were sparkling clean. It looked like the kind of kitchen you'd see photographed for a magazine.

I didn't even realize I was opening the patio doors until I was actually doing it.

When I got inside, I just sort of stood there. There's

nothing stranger than the smell of someone else's house. The scent goes right to your stomach. Mary's house smelled like lemon furniture polish and oatmeal cookies and logs in a fireplace. For some reason it made me want to curl up in the fetal position. I could have slept right there on their kitchen table.

Then all of a sudden my hands were doing things. They opened a cupboard and removed a bowl of cereal. It was weird because I wasn't even hungry. When my hands opened the refrigerator, so much light spilled into the room it felt like I had been caught by the police. My hands removed a quart of milk from the second shelf and set it on the counter. Then they opened up some more cupboards and started rooting around till they found a good bowl. Then they opened about twelve drawers for a spoon. I was getting pretty loud, but for some reason I felt safe.

While I ate the cereal, I totally started crying. I felt so lost I didn't know what to do. My shin was stinging, and when I looked down, I could see blood soaking through my corduroys, just below the knee. My foot felt wet too. I think my one Red Wing was filling with blood.

After I finished my cereal, I set the bowl and spoon in the sink and then I did something completely crazy.

I stole a plate.

It was this huge serving dish hanging above the sink. It had all of these buttercup flowers illustrated around the edge. They were blue and yellow, and just looking at them made you want to start singing some song about a rubber ducky or a kite made of licorice or whatever. I undid the plate from its hook and stuffed it down the front of my pants so half of it was shielding my stomach.

Then I walked into their living room. There was this huge sofa wrapped in plastic and a few overstuffed chairs and a coffee table and bookshelves and lamps and fake trees and embroidered drapes and big stone bowls of pinecones and pictures on the walls.

I was disappointed to find that they didn't have a TV. I'm not sure what I would have done if they did have one; maybe I would have kicked that in too. Or maybe I would have just sat down and watched a late-night movie. I was so disappointed, it made me even more tired. I wanted to lie down right there on the sofa. I even started sort of falling asleep while I was standing up. I had to pinch my face a few times to get my eyes to stay open.

After a minute I finally left through the kitchen patio doors with the plate in my pants.

When I got back to the Fairmont, I opened the

door, set the plate on the passenger's side, and slid into the driver's seat.

My shin was stinging so bad it was almost numb. And my boot was like totally oozing blood every time I hit the gas.

Through the windshield you could see the moon. It looked like something was eating it, little by little.

When I got across the bridge, I started talking to the plate.

"We only have so much time, Mary," I remember saying. "Time will kill you—it really will."

When I turned onto our block, I switched the lights off and stopped the engine. Then I shifted to neutral and coasted into the driveway. I stuffed the plate back down the front of my pants and limped across the porch and opened the door. Welton had greased the hinges a few months before so that they wouldn't squeak when he'd come in late.

I left the car keys on the kitchen table and limped straight to my mom's room. She was sleeping really still, and her room smelled even worse than ever. I just stood there and watched her curtains blowing for a moment. I remember how blue they were. I think it was the first time I had ever noticed them.

It felt like time had stopped, like I was getting free

minutes on earth or something. I remember enjoying that feeling. It was like I was the only one alive who had been given the privilege.

A moment later I heard the door creak behind me. I turned around and my dad was standing in the entrance. He was wearing a three-piece suit. It was gray and it looked too small, like he'd stolen it. You could see where moths had gotten to it. The tie he was wearing was so yellow it almost hurt to look at. He had shaved and there were all these bits of red toilet paper on his neck and face. He had cut himself so many times it almost seemed like he'd done it on purpose.

"What's that?" he asked, pointing at the plate.

His voice wasn't a voice anymore. It was something from a computer. It was like the telephone company had come and replaced it with one of theirs.

"It's a plate," I said.

He made a swallowing sound and adjusted the knot in his tie.

"I got it for Mom," I added.

"She's dead," he said.

He just stood there staring at my mom, but I wouldn't look at her. You couldn't have paid me a million dollars. I was afraid of what I might see, that some other crazy tumor was popping out of her mouth or something.

I just sort of stood there and tried to keep from dropping the plate.

Then he said it again.

"Dead."

One word.

All by itself.

I walked up to him and handed him the plate.

And then I limped down the hall to my room and closed the door.

I sat on the end of my bed for a long time.

My mouth tasted like rust and there were big hunks of glass in my shin.

After a while I just lay down.

I didn't even change my clothes.

I just curled up and fell into a deep, deep sleep.

10

It was about four in the afternoon when I finally got out of bed. I had a terrible headache and I was keenly aware of a searing pain in my shin.

The house was full of murmuring voices. I could practically feel each room getting choked with the hot breath of other people.

I limped to the bathroom and urinated in front of a hospice nurse with big flabby arms. I normally wouldn't ever do anything like that, but I was sort of on autopilot. She was kneeling in the bathtub, trying to break down all of the handicapped equipment. My mom used to sit on this fiberglass bench to shower. Once I walked in on her and she looked almost fake, like my dad had brought her home from a wax museum and thrown her in the shower.

The nurse said, "Excuse me, Steven," and exited the bathroom with some sort of handrail.

I didn't flush, which was also rude, I admit, and decided to hit the refrigerator for a Coke.

As I limped through the living room, I could hear walkie-talkies popping static, but I couldn't quite place where the noise was coming from. In the living room, some severe-looking guy with thick black eyebrows was sitting on the couch. He was wearing a navy blue suit and his hair was combed neatly and he was holding a bouquet of reddish-orange flowers.

I sort of limped over to him.

"Who are you?" I asked.

He stood up and offered his hand.

"Samuel Dames," he replied. "I'm a representative from the funeral home," he added. He was wearing so much cologne I could almost taste it.

I shook his hand. It was cold and hairy.

"You must be Welton," Samuel Dames said. His eyes were all downcast in what seemed like some feeble attempt at humility or compassion or whatever attitude of kindness they try to teach you in funeral school. I didn't even feel like correcting him about mistaking me for my brother.

"I'm very sorry about your mother," he added. "It must have been a long night."

I nodded again.

I could just nod all afternoon and everyone from the hospice center and the funeral home and the morgue and wherever else these people were from

81

would just leave me alone. There must be some unwritten law that says about fifty people have to move into your house when somebody dies. If it weren't for the smell of death clinging to the walls, you might think it was your family's turn to host the monthly neighborhood potluck supper. A little beef and bingo at the Nugents'.

Samuel Dames finally released my hand.

Then all of a sudden I was desperate for a cigarette.

"Hey, do you have a cigarette?" I asked.

"I'm sorry, Welton, but I don't smoke," he replied. I thought it was strange that he hadn't remarked on my shin yet. I mean, even though I was still wearing those corduroys, it was pretty gory. The bloodstain was like a *continent* on my leg.

Samuel Dames's teeth were so white they resembled bathroom tiling. And his eyebrows looked like they might spring off of his forehead and start running across the carpet. I think he might have been wearing a subtle amount of eyeliner, too, but I can't be sure about that.

"Have you seen my dad?" I asked.

"I think he's upstairs talking to the police."

"What are they doing here?" I asked.

"I'm not sure," he replied.

The paper around the flowers crinkled in his hand. I suddenly had this weird thought that Samuel Dames was going to take my dad on a date. I don't know why I thought that. Maybe it was the eyeliner.

I had to leave after I imagined that, so I turned and headed for the kitchen.

"Nice to meet you, Welton," Samuel Dames called after me.

In the kitchen, I opened the fridge and grabbed a can of Coke. I tried to pound it, but I had to stop because I felt like I was going to puke again. It took a minute but I was eventually able to swallow that feeling.

Somehow it was nice in the kitchen. There was the hum of the fridge. And running water. And dishes in the sink. I closed my eyes and tried to focus on that refrigerator hum for a second, but those walkie-talkies kept interrupting.

In the hallway these totally stoic hospital officials were carrying medical equipment out of the house. Their uniforms were so white you had to almost squint. They lugged walkers and IV hangers and those kidney-shaped dishes that you vomit in. There were tubes and chutes and these weird, skin-colored things that looked like they had no purpose whatsoever. They hauled monitors and bedside rails and machines that looked more like they belonged in a mechanic's garage than in someone's bedroom.

Man, my head was pounding.

A few of the hospice nurses squeezed my shoulder as I passed them on the way to the staircase. One of them pointed to my bloody shin and I nodded. They were like these big sad dolphins gliding around on Rollerblades or something. What's weird is that I don't think I ever knew their names. Not even one. They would say these totally selfless things to me, like, "If you ever need anything, dot, dot, dot," or, "You look tired, sweetheart. Can I get you a blah, blah, blah?" I'd never spoken to them, though. Instead I'd count the weird hairs on their chins or I'd imagine them blow-drying their armpits in the nude or whatever. I know that's horrible, but this is about being honest, right?

Welton was downstairs blaring Bottomside. It was so loud you could practically feel it vibrating in the soles of your feet. He was probably going against the computer on PlayStation. I imagined him playing this snowboard game. I could just see it: he had burned his daily wake-and-bake and turned on Bottomside with the remote and dug out the joystick thing from underneath his laundry heap. I thought about going down there, but I didn't. For some reason I was afraid that it was actually Dantly down in the basement, that Dantly was my brother now. The thought made me so tired I had to lean against the railing in the stairwell.

I could hear walkie-talkies again. They were coming from behind the door to my dad's room. I put my ear to the door and listened.

A cop was talking. He was saying how strange it was that there was no destruction to the lock on the front door to the electronics shop. No evidence of breaking and entering. Only seventeen busted TVs, some point-of-sale graffiti, and a smashed bird from a cuckoo clock. No apparent theft. No damage to the cash register. Only vandalism.

My dad kept saying, "I know, I know. I don't understand," and things of that nature.

I opened the door and there were like four cops standing around. Man, they didn't look like cops. They looked more like guys who were *pretending* to be cops. Like community theater cops or something.

My dad was sitting on the end of his bed with his face in his hands. He was still wearing his moth-eaten suit with the yellow tie. And there were still the bits of bloody toilet paper scabbed on his jaws from where he had cut himself shaving. It sort of looked like flies were eating his face. The bed was so perfect it seemed like the cops had forced him to make it at gunpoint.

Above the bed there was this totally haunted-looking painting of a clown with balloons in its cheeks. The clown had an upside-down smile, and he was holding this huge umbrella. It was raining sideways, so the umbrella was useless. I had never seen the painting before.

The plate from Mary's house had been set on top of my parents' dresser. There was a rubber band and some loose change scattered in the middle.

The cops stared at me and I stared back at them. The four of them looked the same to me. Same haircuts. Same meaty forearms. Same blank white faces.

My dad was now staring at me like he was hungry, like they had been starving him or something. Then this one cop spoke.

"Son," he said, "are you aware that your leg is bleeding?"

"Yes," I said.

The cops all looked at each other, all concerned and suspicious. One of them turned his walkie-talkie off and went, "Son, where were you last night?" I thought it was funny how they were all calling me *son*. My dad didn't even have the balls to use my name or even some sort of lame, sexless pronoun, but those cops could totally like rattle off *son*.

"I did it," I said.

I figured I'd cut to the chase.

I turned to my dad. His mouth looked collapsed, like one of the cops had smashed it in with the butt of his gun. He was making these weird noises like he was choking to death, but he wasn't. He was actually crying.

"What did you do exactly?" another cop asked. His voice was higher than the first one's.

"I kicked the TVs in," I said. "All seventeen of 'em." Man, my hands were shaking like crazy. "So take me away," I added.

But no one would move. The cops just stood there with their hands on their belts.

So I just stood there too.

The fact was it was four-thirty in the afternoon and my mom was dead.

I never even saw them wheel her out.

11

So before I continue with the story part, I have to tell you about something weird that happened last night with Shannon.

We were sitting at this table in the TV lounge and it was pretty late. We had been talking about this play he gave me by Sam Shepard called *Buried Child*. It was a pretty intense play that deals with this family in southern Illinois and all of their creepy secrets. I was telling him how I thought it was actually the corn that was beckoning Vince, the young hero of the play, homeward. I was explaining my theory in great detail when Shannon leaned forward and kissed me on the mouth. It wasn't just like something men do in Europe, either, where I understand a kiss hello and goodbye happens all the time—this was different. It involved an open mouth and his tongue and saliva and it lasted like ten seconds, which is sort of an eternity when it comes to a kiss.

The first thing I said when it was over was, "Whoa."

Then he said, "Yeah, whoa."

"Um. Are you like gay?" I asked, wiping my mouth.

"Nuh-uh," he said. "Are you?"

"Nuh-uh," I answered.

Then we just sat there for a second. The new Blue Grouper named Daryl Francis was asleep on the sofa in front of the TV and this Claymation Christmas special was on about this elf named Herbie who wants to grow up to be a dentist. I watched Daryl for a second to make sure that he wasn't just fake-sleeping and he wasn't, thank God.

"Well, that was weird," Shannon said. "See you tomorrow." Then he got up from the table and walked away.

I said, "See you tomorrow," too and just sat there listening to the lights buzzing above me.

Jesus, that was weird.

When I got back to my room, I brushed my teeth like four times and I couldn't stop touching my lips.

So I have *no idea* what to think about all of that. I mean, that sort of changes *everything* between me and Shannon, right? In a way I hope it doesn't, because he's my best friend at Burnstone Grove, but how could it not?

"Anything new?" Mrs. Leene asked at our session this morning, and I almost told her, I really did, but I couldn't. Instead of telling her about what happened, I made up some story about how I walked in on this Gray Grouper named Mike Seminaro masturbating in the men's bathroom.

"Did it upset you?" Mrs. Leene asked.

"No," I said. "I just wish he would do that in his room."

I'm such a liar, it makes me sick. But I promise I'm not lying about any of the stuff that happened—I swear I'm not.

I wonder what it's going to be like at dinner when I see Shannon Lynch again. Maybe we'll just act like nothing happened at all. And then again maybe he'll try to kiss me with romantic force or something.

So back to my mom's death.

My mom my mom my mom my mom my mom . . .

The day after she died, the cops took me to the hospital and this totally detached, nonchalant plastic surgeon removed about twenty pieces of glass from my right shin. The pain was like something mechanical boring through my body. I had to get a tetanus shot, too, which made my shoulder sore for like three days.

At the funeral my stitches were itching like crazy, but it didn't bother me much because I was like totally tripping on the codeine they'd prescribed for the pain.

They cremated my mom and stuffed her ashes into a pine box and put an eight-by-ten photo next to it. In the photo she was wearing too much makeup and it made me want to smash it with my fist.

During the service, everyone talked about all the things she had done for the pediatrics ward at the hospital.

"She helped my boy Brian," one anonymous woman said.

One man directed his testimonial to my dad. He said, "I lost my little girl to leukemia and your wife really helped us through a difficult time. Elizabeth passed in peace and Mary Lee Nugent was a big part of that."

Once I looked over at Welton and he was wiping his nose. I couldn't tell if he was crying or on nasal spray.

When the priest announced that there would be a moment of silence for those of us who were too shy to share a special memory or speak on Mary's behalf, Welton started singing "The Star-Spangled Banner." He like sang the entire song and everyone just let him do it. When he was finished, the priest made the sign of the cross and said something about grief and how through prayer Jesus and His Holy Father and all the other various gods and monsters of Catholicism would eventually lead everyone who loved my mom to a place of peace. Like if we did our Catholic duty to suffer and pray and take communion, we'd all wind up in some sacred pasture with cows and turtledoves and picnic baskets.

Aunt Ricky—my mom's overweight, hard-core Christian sister—was crying so hard you would've thought she was being attacked by wasps.

After his rendition of "The Star-Spangled Banner," Welton just stared straight ahead at the altar as if he were waiting for Jesus to climb down off the cross and escape with him. They would load up in Dantly's Skylark and the three of them would go score some Ex in Cedar Rapids. Jesus would like totally ride shotgun and scout for cops.

At the banquet hall, everyone was gorging themselves. My aunt Ricky ate about four plates of roast beef with horseradish. Lyman Singer never actually sat down. He just stood by the pan of chicken wings, refilling his plate. His whole beard was totally slathered with barbecue sauce. Even the *priest* couldn't get enough of the baked beans. I'd never seen someone eat so many baked beans in my life. And he dumped about half a bottle of ketchup on them, too. Man, there's nothing like a funeral to get the old salivary glands juiced up.

On our way home, my dad handed me this letter that he'd received from the gifted school. It was addressed to him and my mom, and it said that I was eligible to graduate early if I took a summer English course. According to the letter, it had to be a creative writing course offered by one of the local high schools. The gifted school is weird like that. If they think you're ready to graduate, they'll let you out early. To tell you the truth, I think it's all based on your SATs, because I took them spring of my sophomore year and I pretty much topped the charts, thus the letter. They probably figured I would get into Harvard or Dartmouth or one of those schools with vines all over the walls.

When I got home, I went down to the basement and stood in front of Welton's door. I knew he was in there again, because you could hear Bottomside playing. He had walked home by himself, ignoring all of our relatives' offers to give him a ride. He was probably in there getting stoned and playing Sims. I almost knocked like thirty times—I would raise my hand and everything—but for some reason I couldn't make a fist. I have no idea what I was going to say to him.

I don't know what I felt at my mom's funeral. I was pretty sad, I'll admit that, but I wasn't like *bereft* or anything. Like my aunt Ricky was *bereft*. After the service, she couldn't even get herself out of the pew. My dad and his brother Truman had to lift her out like she was an elk they'd shot up in Canada or something. Mrs. Leene says that everyone grieves differently, that sorrow and anger manifest themselves in strange ways because of how our minds are actually designed to protect us from those feelings. I will say this: I wish I could have cried then. I think if I could have had a good cry, things might have gotten better somehow.

12

So it was Christmas yesterday, and this Blue Grouper named Trevor Butz led an hour of caroling with his acoustic guitar. He's not a bad guitarist. He exhibited several different strumming techniques, and I was impressed.

"He can do bar chords," Shannon noticed, and he's the one who would know.

I was surprised about how many kids actually sang along. "The Little Drummer Boy" was like this huge hit.

I basically sat next to Shannon and sort of sang under my breath. He sang louder, as he seems to be afraid of nothing.

We didn't talk about the kiss, and things actually felt sort of normal between us.

Two days ago, they gave everyone forty dollars and loaded us up on a chartered school bus and took us to this mall in the middle of nowhere to purchase a Secret Santa gift. While we were on the bus, Dr. Shays passed around a backpack that had everyone's names written on individual pieces of paper. We all reached into it and selected a name, and that's who we had to buy a present for. Of all people, I selected Silent Starla, who, for some reason I still can't quite fathom, hates me with a vengeance.

In the mall I was surprised to discover that there was a pretty decent indie-rock record store and I wound up buying her two CDs by this band called Cat Power and that Interpol CD that I was telling you about before. Cat Power's really this woman Chan Marshall, and she has this beautiful voice and sings these sad songs that will melt just about anyone.

After the caroling, everyone exchanged Secret Santa gifts. This Red Grouper named Barry Castro gave me an electric toothbrush, which is cool, except now I'm paranoid that I have bad breath or something.

"It's s'posed to be really good for your gums," Barry said after he watched me open it. He's sort of chubby and has this black hair that somehow looks more like a wig than hair. He also stutters occasionally, which makes me feel sorry for him.

"Thanks," I said to him.

"It really is s'posed to be good for your gums," he said, and then headed toward this white-chocolate sculpture Nativity scene.

When Silent Starla opened her CDs, she looked at them for a moment and said, "Who's this?"

I said, "Just these bands I like."

She studied the CD covers for a second, and said, "Then you should have gotten them for yourself," and handed them back to me.

What a fucking bitch, I thought. *What a fucking ungrateful, mean-spirited bitch!*

Later on at the eggnog bowl, I went up to her. "I thought maybe you'd like these," I said, reoffering the CDs. To be honest, I wanted to say something like four thousand times more potent than that, but I couldn't for some reason. Maybe it was the Christmas spirit holding me back.

Then Starla said something weird. She said, "Killers listen to that kind of music."

I said, "They do?"

"Killers and speed skaters."

Speed skaters? I thought, and I was going to ask her about what that meant, but then she took the CDs back and there was even one moment where I think she was trying to be nice to me because she said something else, which was, "You remind me of this guy I used to know in Gary who said interesting things once in a while. He was tall too."

Then she downed her eggnog and went back to her room with the CDs I'd bought her.

To stay with the holiday theme, I should also tell you about this card I received from my dad today. It was a huge shock because of all the dramatic stuff that has happened between us. Most of it follows, trust me.

Anyway, it was a Christmas card and there was a big red Santa on the front and when I opened it, on the right side it said *Have a Merry Christmas, Ho Ho Ho* in green ink — it was part of the card. On the left side, in pencil, my dad wrote:

> Steven,
>> I'm sorry about stuff.
>> I hope you're doing okay.
>> Love,
>>> Dad

He's pretty much all alone in the house now, except for Aunt Ricky, who's been staying there with him. I don't think he's gone back to work at the shop yet. It's going on five months now. The last time we spoke, he was talking about selling the house and moving to Maryland. He said there was a job opportunity there with his old gypsum-board ceiling-slat business.

"A move might be good," he said.

His voice sounded small and worn out.

When I hung up the phone in the Burnstone Grove common room, I felt really alien from him, like there's just too much distance between us to get back to the way things used to be before my mom's illness and the whole thing with Welton. That phone conversation happened like a month ago, and we haven't spoken since. So the card was definitely a surprise.

Mrs. Leene thinks he's still ashamed because he was so helpless in the face of my mom's cancer.

"He's probably still devastated," she said. "It might take a very long time before he's able to be the person you expect him to be."

Person.

I said, "He's like this big blob of meat."

"You should give him a chance, Steve."

The problem with Mrs. Leene is that she's always right. When you think about it, I guess that's not really such a bad thing. It must be hard to date a person like that, though, and I said as much to her this morning.

"It must be hard to date you," I said.

"Why do you say that, Steven?" she asked.

"Because you're like this genius."

She laughed when I said that, and now I know she

knows that I like her. But I won't wander off the subject too much. Not just yet.

So what happened after my mom died was this:

In order for the shop to collect insurance, my dad had to press charges against me, which meant I had to appear in juvenile court.

Remember Welton's brown slacks that I was telling you about before? Well, I own a pair of those too, and they came with a matching suit jacket. My mom found the polyester-blend suits on the clearance rack at J.C. Penney. Mine smelled like compact-car upholstery, and the first time I put it on, I was paranoid that it had some weird chemical relationship to heat, that if exposed to the sun, it would burst into flames or something.

So that's what I wore in court: the brown suit with a pair of wingtip shoes, a white shirt, and a striped tie. I probably looked like some Young Republican.

The courthouse in downtown Foote is this old limestone building next to the library. I never imagined that I would have any reason to go into this building, and yet there I was.

Just over the steps there's this huge American flag that they put up after 9/11. I guess they don't have any plans of taking it down, even though Foote, Iowa, had absolutely nothing to do with that tragedy.

During the ride over, it was so quiet you could hear

the keys jingling in the ignition. My dad was driving like he was lost on some forgotten country road. He kept making this face like he didn't quite know where he was going.

We parked in front of the library, and as soon as we entered the courthouse, he slipped into the bathroom.

"Just a sec, okay?" he said, and sneaked away.

In the rotunda area, there were all of these huge old oil paintings of former American presidents. While I was checking out the Grover Cleveland portrait, this well-dressed woman with glasses approached me.

"Are you Steven?" she asked.

Her name was Lynette something-or-other and she was from Children's Services. She was forty-ish, I'd guess, and sort of pretty in that no-makeup, lesbian way. She explained that she would sit with me during the hearing so I would feel supported.

"So are you like my lawyer?" I asked.

"Sort of," she said. "The court assigned me to your case. But since you've already confessed to everything, I'm basically just a formality. But I'm happy to answer any questions if things get confusing in there. They're actually waiting for us right now," she said kindly.

Lynette then escorted me to the hearing room, which was this sort of blank white room with a big glossy wooden table. She sat next to me. There was a pitcher of water in the middle of the table with some Dixie cups.

On the other side of the table, my dad was huddling with his lawyer, this guy named Dave who had driven all the way from Cedar Rapids. I thought it was weird how he'd sneaked out of the bathroom when I wasn't looking.

"Hi, Steven," Dave said to me. I had met him at the shop once.

"Hey," I said back.

He has a son who is Welton's age. He's apparently attending Drake University on an academic scholarship.

My dad was wearing his gray, moth-eaten suit and yellow tie again. For a second it felt like he and Dave were totally planning to kill me or something.

"Thirsty?" Lynette asked.

I nodded and she poured both of us Dixie cups of water. It wasn't exactly cold and tasted chlorinated.

That's when this bailiff guy entered the room with the judge. The bailiff was pretty weird-looking. He had a shaved head and wore these yellow safety glasses, like he'd just returned from a rigorous go of it at the Foote gun club or something. The judge was pretty old, at least sixty-something, and his black gown made him look like some sort of geriatric Halloween creature in drag.

The bailiff then asked everyone to rise and said a few insubstantial courtroom-type things and then, in this unbearably painful five-part move, the judge sat down at the head of the table.

After he got settled, he made this hand gesture that was obviously our cue to sit, so we all did so in unison— almost like we were in church or something.

The room smelled like bleach and furniture polish.

While Dave cataloged the list of damages to the shop, the judge kept staring at me and shaking his head. I noticed that his hands constantly trembled and he had to swallow a lot.

For some reason, Dave started to look really fake to me. Fake like wood. Fake like one of those Santas at the mall.

While he read down his list of damages to the store, my dad kept looking at me like he was sort of apologizing.

I even said, "What?" once, but he didn't respond. Everyone at the table sort of held their breath until the old judge said, "Resume, please."

The rest of the details of the hearing are sort of boring, so I won't take you through it. The whole thing ended with my guilty plea and Lynette saying something about my honesty about coming forth during such a difficult time.

The bottom line is that instead of sending me off to live with the rapists and murderers at the Ethan Allen Home in Wasaw, Wisconsin, the judge said he was sympathetic because of my mom dying and all and he assigned a community service task instead. Before he let me go, he warned me that I was on the wrong path.

"You're on the wrong path, Steven Nugent," he said.

I looked at my dad again, who was sort of staring at his hands.

"It's time you take a self-inventory and think about what you've done," I heard the judge say.

I just sat there and nodded. Or at least I *think* I nodded.

"I don't want to see you in here again, is that clear?" he said.

"Yes, sir," I said.

Then he sort of pulled at the loose flesh around these totally hound dog–looking jowls of his and he asked me if I had anything I wished to say.

"No," I said. "Not really."

"Are you even a bit sorry for your actions, young man?" he asked.

"Yes," I lied. "I'm sorry."

"Perhaps you should tell your father that."

My dad was still staring at his hands. The ceiling fan churned above us slowly.

"I'm sorry, Dad," I said.

It was suddenly unbearably hot. My brown suit was totally strangling me.

At the steps to the courtroom, Lynette said goodbye to me and gave me her card, saying that I should give her a call if I ever needed anything. Then I said goodbye to Dave, and he and my dad hugged for what seemed like way too long, and then we got back in the Fairmont and drove home. I rolled my window down and let my arm hang down the side of the car.

"What should we have for dinner?" he asked after we went over the bridge.

"I don't know," I said. "I'm not so hungry."

"I was thinking about ordering Domino's."

For some reason the thought of eating pizza made me sick, so I didn't respond.

When we got home, he went straight to bed and fell asleep in his clothes.

13.

So that night was a strange one. It felt like my body was starting to do things on its own, sort of without thought, kind of like my hands in Mary Mills's kitchen, but now it was spreading everywhere.

I couldn't sleep so I sat at my desk and smoked a few cigarettes. I tried some more Robitussin because I thought it would help me get drowsy, but it only made me feel edgier somehow.

So that's when I decided to sneak into my dad's room with the electric razor. It was probably around three A.M. or something. I had heard Welton come in a few hours earlier. I think he fell down in the kitchen. I was going to go downstairs and see if he was okay, but I got that creepy feeling that he was turning into Dantly again so I didn't.

My dad had fallen asleep in his suit. His yellow tie was all wrapped around his neck. His knees were tucked into his chest; he was sleeping like a man who'd been beaten.

All types of random stuff had been strewn around my parents' room. Stuff like T-shirts and church slacks and half-eaten TV dinners and strings to pajama bottoms and orphaned slippers and dirty socks and fallen curtains and a dented lampshade and like a dozen multicolored felt-tip pens and *TV Guide*s and a few of my mom's old nightgowns and this totally ominous-looking ball-peen hammer.

My dad's dresser drawers were all open, too, as was his closet and window. It was like he'd been searching for some weird animal he had been hiding. Maybe like some furry little creature to replace my mom. A guinea pig or a gerbil or something of that nature.

What made it even worse were the mosquitoes. They were hovering near the middle of the ceiling by what seemed like the dozens. And it was obvious that they had feasted on my dad, as there were little bite marks all over his neck and hands.

He woke up just after I clicked the razor on, but I did manage to mow off a pretty decent chunk before he started choking me.

His hands were around my throat in this way that made me think that he had been fantasizing about choking me for a long time. The razor landed on the floor and continued buzzing, which was pretty annoying. With my feet I could feel his shoes under the covers.

I could also feel that plate that I had stolen from Mary Mills's house. *What is he doing with all this stuff under the covers?* I thought. He was like *sleeping* with it.

My dad smelled sort of like mustard, which was probably due to the fact that in the bed I also discovered a thing of Hellmann's. I wanted to grab it and squirt it in his eyes, but I couldn't reach it.

There was this scary moment in which I think part of me actually wanted my dad to kill me.

In this totally whispery voice, I even told him to.

"Do it, Dad," I said. "It's okay. Do it."

I know that's almost one-hundred percent Blue Groupery of me, but that's honestly how I felt.

At some point I totally left my body. I was hovering near the ceiling with all the mosquitoes. Man, the me in my parents' bed was in pretty bad shape. His face was so blue it was almost black. I thought about a lot of stuff in that moment. Things like finding fossils at the national forest when I was a kid. Things like using a metal detector for the first time. Things like skipping rocks on the Mississippi. All this stuff we used to do together when things were still okay.

Then the bed collapsed and it was over.

I'd forgotten how strong my dad was. He played football in high school—middle linebacker, actually—but you would never have known it looking at him. He was also in the Marines for a while. But he looked so thin and tired anymore, always falling asleep in his La-Z-Boy, half-eaten bowls of cereal at his feet, his little potbelly sneaking over his pajama bottoms, his bald shins.

After we were thoroughly off the bed and panting like zoo creatures, my dad reached over and turned off the razor.

"She wouldn't let me wash her hair anymore," he said, trying to catch his wind. Man, his breath was so mustardy it almost made me sick. "No more washing . . ." he added, trailing off.

Then he cried on the floor for like ten minutes, and I just sat there next to him holding my neck and panting. My Adam's apple felt like it had been pulled out and replaced by a nine-volt battery or something.

I took the razor from him and stood. My legs felt weak and rubbery. I had to use the dresser to keep my balance.

The picture of the clown with balloons in its cheeks had fallen off the wall. It was upside-down now and its frown was a weird, ghoulish smile.

After I walked out of the room, I took the razor into the bathroom and shaved my head. I don't expect you to understand why I did that; God knows I still don't. Like I said, things were just happening by themselves.

I started buzzing everything off in front, just above my forehead. Then I moved around to the sides and sort of did a lot of guesswork in the back.

I never realized how big my ears were. It made me uglier than I already was, but I didn't care.

The other day the Blue Grouper Jimmy Smallhorn said that your ears and the tip of your nose are the only things that keep growing when you get old. Maybe when I get old, I'll have these total elephant ears and it will be cool to the younger generation.

When I was through shaving my head, I ran cold water over my skull.

That felt pretty good, I must say.

14

The following morning, I started my community service assignment.

What I had to do was paint a brick wall. It was about thirty feet long and fifteen feet high. It faced the river, and someone had spray-painted FUCK ON THE INTERNET in five-foot red letters across the middle.

My community service supervisor, who I will describe in greater detail in just a minute, told me that the city was leasing out the wall for advertising space. Apparently, in the near future some casino boat would travel up and down the Mississippi all day. The wall would make for good marketing, so FUCK ON THE INTERNET had to get covered up before the owners of the building could start showing the wall to potential advertisers.

I guess it was all part of this citywide effort to clean up the riverfront area. In the past few years, it's gotten pretty sketchy, with vandalism and these fake Caucasian gangs acting all rap video.

My supervisor supplied me with the paint and a pack of rollers. He and a few friends who I never saw had erected scaffolding so I could reach the top of the wall.

When I arrived at the work site, it was already around eighty-five degrees and the Mississippi smelled heinous. Dragonflies were darting here and there, and mosquitoes were pretty much omnipresent.

The supervisor guy was wearing a red tank top and Bermuda shorts. He was pretty pasty—even pastier than me—and his fat arms were wet from the humidity.

I was wearing a pair of Welton's carpenter jeans and this long-sleeved T-shirt featuring a picture of a squirrel with human testicles. Apparently Dantly had paid some computer specialist from the nursing home to download the image off the Internet and then he and Welton had T-shirts made at some copy shop in Foote.

The reason I was wearing that particular shirt is that in general I can't *stand* wearing short sleeves. I don't care how hot it gets. Having bare arms makes me feel like I'm trapped in the locker room with a bunch of hairy jocks or something.

My community service supervisor looked at me and went, "You the Nugent boy?"

I nodded.

"Steve, right?" he offered politely.

I nodded again.

"Jerry Willems," he said, extending his hand. We shook. My guess is that he was around fifty years old. For some reason he sort of reminded me of a gym coach. Maybe it's because he wore a referee's whistle around his neck, which he never used. It sort of made me paranoid that at any moment he might blow into it and make me drop to the ground to do pushups or burpees or something. In general, I would describe him as being abundantly fleshy.

I palmed my skull a few times, which was turning into a pretty cool new habit, I must say. It was cold and sort of leathery-feeling.

"So here's what's what," he said. "You'll work for three hours and then we'll take a lunch break, come back, and work another three. The whole thing's gotta be blue. If you work hard, you should be able to get it done. Paint's mixed up and ready to stick. She might take more than one coat, so you best get to it."

He was a pretty stern guy, definitely not to be messed with.

Before I started painting, I walked over to the bag I'd packed that morning. It was my dad's old Marine Corps bag. Inside it were a few pairs of underwear, some T-shirts, a thing of Old Spice deodorant, a tube of toothpaste and my toothbrush, my Discman and head-phones, a few packs of double-A batteries, two fresh bottles of Robitussin that I'd stolen from Welton's room, three packs of Camel Lights (also stolen from Welton's room), four or five of my favorite CDs, and a black per-manent marker. To tell you the truth, I have no idea why I packed a black permanent marker. At the time it just seemed like one of those things you would need.

Because of what had happened the night before, I'd decided that I wouldn't be staying at home anymore.

I grabbed a pack of cigarettes and put them in my back pocket. I also took a bite of a candy bar that I had bought on my way over. I was pretty hungry and I had no idea how I was going to feed myself. I only had like thirty bucks that I'd scrabbled together. I could totally feel that Jerry Willems guy watching me. When I fin-ished with the bag, I stepped up to the wall, dipped my roller in the paint, and got to work. The wall was pretty moldy, and in addition to the dragonflies and mosquitoes that I described earlier, there were all these bugs swarming in and out of the cracks. The paint fumes were pretty potent, too, and after a while I started to feel a little stoned.

At some point, maybe after like a half an hour or so, Jerry Willems came over with what appeared to be a long broomstick.

"You should attach this to the roller," he offered. "Might make things a heckuva lot easier."

I took his advice and he was right—it totally made it easier.

Jerry Willems watched me for a few minutes, saying things like "Not bad technique" and "Use your legs more," and then he left me alone. He pretty much just stayed over by where he had parked his big red pickup truck and talked on his cell phone.

For the next two hours, I just zoned out and painted the wall. My Adam's apple was still sore from getting choked, and every time I swallowed, I was reminded of my dad's face over mine, how swollen and weird it looked, how lost we both were. I wanted to feel bad about everything that had happened—I really did—but more than anything, I just felt sort of blank. Even when I thought about my mom, I felt blank.

I had to stop painting a few times because my stitches were itching like crazy. I had this weird urge to pull them out and just let my shin bleed everywhere.

While I was down on a knee, Jerry Willems came back over.

"What's wrong with your leg?" he asked.

"A few days ago I fell on some glass," I lied.

"Ouch," he said. "How many stitches?"

"Like sixty-some," I replied. I really had no idea how many the doctor had sewn into my shin, but that sounded right for some reason.

"Well, I just came over to tell you it's your lunch break. There are sandwiches and pop in my truck."

We walked over to his truck, and I ate like four ham sandwiches and drank three orange Fantas.

When I was just about to head back to the wall, Jerry Willems came around from the other side of his truck holding two baseball mitts.

"Have a catch?" he asked, hiking up his Bermuda shorts.

I said, "Like a *catch* catch?"

"Sure," he said. "Get fifty feet between a coupla fellas and let her fly."

I thought for a second.

"It's good for clearin' the head," he added.

"Maybe not," I said.

"Okay," he said, and turned and walked back toward his truck.

116

I felt sort of bad rejecting him like that. I mean, I know he was just trying to be nice to me. I guess I just wasn't in the mood for a catch.

I went back to work on the wall and started thinking about that letter from the gifted school. I had been planning on going over to Carroll on Monday and signing up for a summer-school writing class. I had never been very interested in writing, which is pretty ironic because of what you're reading right now. The only book I've ever really liked was this one called *The Basketball Diaries,* by Jim Carroll, which is about this white kid in New York City who's this totally amazing basketball player but he doesn't even care because he's all into shooting heroin and getting into trouble with his friends. It turns out that Jim Carroll really *did* live on the streets of New York City and he really *was* this talented basketball player and he really *did* have this whole love affair with heroin and other various urban drugs. Man, that's the only kind of book I like—one that's so real you want to find out everything there is to know about the person who wrote it, like how tall he is and what kind of music he likes and whether or not he really went through all the stuff he was writing about.

It took me the rest of the day, and I wound up climbing up on that rickety old scaffolding, but I eventually got the whole wall painted. I was pretty tired at the end, but it was that good kind of tired, when you feel like you've actually accomplished something.

When I was finished, Jerry Willems came over and shook my hand.

"Not bad," he said. "Good luck with everything, and stay outta trouble."

I nodded, grabbed my bag, and headed into downtown Foote.

15.

So it was official.

My temporary homelessness had begun.

But before I go on with that, I have to tell you what just happened here at Burnstone Grove.

That Silent Starla girl just came into my room and sat on my bed. Just like that. She didn't even knock— she just sort of waltzed right through the threshold. I was at my desk with my pen and my composition book, crossing out things and rereading what I think will be chapter 14.

"Hey," she said.

"Hey," I said back.

"What's that?" she asked, pointing to my journal. She had a lot of dark eyeliner on, which made her eyes look spooky and beautiful at the same time.

"Oh, it's nothing," I said. "I'm just writing this thing."

"Is that a diary?"

"Sort of."

"Don't let anyone see it."

"I keep it hidden," I said, which is true. I keep it in this hidden pocket in my mom's old suitcase that I brought here.

Then she sort of bounced a little on the bed and said, "So what's been up?"

"Not much," I answered. "What's been up with you?"

"I'm just chillin'," she responded, which was weird because that's sort of homeboy or something, and I've never seen that side of her.

Then there was this long pause. You could hear the fluorescent light tube over my desk buzzing. Silent Starla sort of gave me this look. It was half-bored, half-mischievous.

I said, "What?"

She bounced a few more times and said, "So, I really like all that music you gave me."

"Really?" I said.

"Really," she said. "That Cat Power chick is pretty good. I'm mean, she's sad as shit and sort of lost in that please-come-home-with-me-I'd-like-to-sleep-with-you-now-get-the-fuck-out-of-my-life kind of way. I mean, I'm right, right?"

"Totally," I said.

"And Interpol. They're sort of post-punk but kind of mysterious and they can rock petty hard when they want to. I like that song 'Roland.'"

"Yeah, 'Roland' rocks."

Then she shot me another one of those looks and said something that totally caught me by surprise, which was, "So, do you wanna make out?"

I said, "Make out?"

"Uh-huh."

Inside I was like, "Whoa," but I didn't say that. In fact, I didn't say anything. I almost stopped breathing, if truth be told. My hands suddenly got all clammy and I started making fists to hide this fact. She looked so good sort of bouncing at the end of my bed like that.

Then Silent Starla said, "I mean, we don't have to."

"No, I'd like to," I said. "I'd just feel a little weird, I guess."

"Why?"

"Because of Shannon."

Silent Starla said, *"Shannon?"*

"Yeah," I said, "Shannon Lynch."

"What about him?"

"I think he likes you."

"Well, I don't like him."

"Oh," I said. "You don't?"

"No," she answered. "And besides, everybody knows he's gay."

"Really?"

"I mean, it's not like in-your-face obvious or anything, but he is."

"How do you know?"

"Because since he's been here, he's tried to kiss like four different guys."

I was pretty shocked to hear that. I guess mostly because it made me feel like a statistic. I was Number Five.

Silent Starla then said, "So come here, Gray Grouper," and patted the spot next to her on the bed.

I went over and sat next to her, and she undid my fists and sort of pressed her thumbs into my palms.

"So, is your name really Starla?" I asked.

"It's really Sinead. But I changed it to Starla last year after I dropped acid for the first time. You can call me Sinead if you want."

"I like Starla," I said.

"Good," she said. "Lean toward me."

"Okay," I said, but I just sort of froze there—I was really nervous. But she sensed it and helped me out by sort of placing her hand between my shoulder blades and gently pushing me toward her. We totally made out for like fifteen minutes. Her mouth tasted like cigarettes and Cherry Coke, which, as strange as it sounds, is a surprisingly good combination. It was mostly French kissing and some rubbing on thigh areas, which all felt pretty masterful, I must say.

So I think I'm in love with Silent Starla, who isn't all that silent after all. In group she hardly ever talks, and in the cafeteria she just sort of stares off in this dreamy way. She's from Oak Park, Illinois, and when she left my room, she said, "We can go together, but I won't fuck you without a condom. I like your eyes."

Then she left, just as mysteriously as she had appeared.

I hope that we have sex as soon as possible.

I hope I hope I hope I hope I hope I hope I hope . . .

I just had to say that, and now I will stop complaining about my virgin curse and I'll return to the subject of my temporary homelessness in downtown Foote.

Even though I had eaten those ham sandwiches during my community service lunch, I was starving again. I stopped at a diner near the Century Civic Center. It's this totally old-fashioned, fifties-looking place called Jack Palomino's. The booths are all red vinyl and riddled with cigarette burns, and the old-fashioned jukebox isn't even plugged in and there's a crack in the glass. Another thing that I'd like to describe are the walls, which at the time were plastered with movie posters. Man, it seemed that everywhere you looked in downtown Foote, there were movie posters. Three overly tan studs in sunglasses. Four noble-looking women staring off into the horizon. Some old Scottish guy in a Lamborghini smiling knowingly at a swimsuit model with fake breasts. He's like an international spy or whatever and she's the sexy scientist with the Transylvanian accent.

There were about three people, all in different booths. The air conditioner was obviously broken, as a pair of matching fans whirled feebly in opposite corners.

This middle-aged waitress with dyed red hair sort of limped over to my table. Both of her knees were wrapped in Ace bandages and she seemed pretty bored about things.

I ordered a hot dog with extra crispy French fries and a glass of ginger ale.

In the far corner, there was this little blond girl sitting in a booth by herself. She was probably ten or eleven, and she was so dirty it was like someone had made her up that way for Halloween. She was exhibiting some pretty restless behavior. First she was sitting, then she'd get up and walk around and slide into the other side of the booth. She'd stay that way for a minute, playing with the salt and pepper shakers or whatever was there, and then she'd get up on her knees and stare out the window. She never sat still. Sometimes when she was at the window, she'd breathe on the glass and draw initials in the steam with her finger.

Every few minutes, the waitress would tell her to keep her feet off the seat and the little girl would take them down, but as soon as the waitress would turn her head, she would put her feet right back up on the seat. A true rebel in the making.

Besides the girl, there was this elderly, white-haired lady reading a paperback, and this heavyset guy wearing spandex shorts and a mesh tank top. He was sitting right in front of one of the fans, and I think it was making the whole place smell funny.

I was pretty beat and in need of a shower. Where this would take place, I had no idea. My shoulders ached from all that painting, and the back of my neck felt raw and sunburned. I wanted to take off my Red Wing boots, but I knew I would have been thrown out. I had my dad's Marine Corps bag under my legs, and I kept checking it nervously as if the few things that I had packed might have dematerialized or something.

The little girl kept eyeing my hot dog. At a closer look, I could see that she had been eating mustard and ketchup packets. That dirt on her face was probably dried condiments. She had neatly lined up the empty packets on the table in rows of three. My guess was that she probably got them from the McDonald's down the street.

For a second I thought the waitress was the little girl's mother because of how she was telling her to keep her feet off the booth seat. I was even going to ask her if they were related, but the waitress disappeared into the kitchen.

When I looked back at the girl, she wasn't there. I scanned the diner. I met eyes with the old woman reading the paperback. Her mouth was sort of half-open, and she looked like she felt sorry for everyone and everything. Her eyes were gray the way wood goes gray, like an old rowboat.

"Hey," a voice suddenly called to me over my shoulder.

I turned and it was the little girl. She was sitting in the booth behind me. A pair of dirty elbows and a head. Up close you could see that she had a few freckles and that one of her front teeth was chipped. She was wearing a T-shirt that had a picture of a pickle on the front. Just a pickle and nothing else. Like her face, the T-shirt was stained here and there with ketchup and mustard.

"Hey," I said back to her.

"You gonna eat all that?" she asked.

I gave her the rest of my hot dog, and she wolfed it down in about three bites.

"Why you bald? You got bugs or somethin'?" the girl asked between mouthfuls.

I was like, "Um, no."

"You a skinhead?"

"I'm a Crip," I said. "I just got in from Cali."

"You ain't no Crip," she said. "Lemme feel it."

Before I could say anything, she was palming my head. She felt it for a second and said, "It's like a dog's tongue." Then she took her hand back. "Like this German shepherd I used to know. Carlos."

I went, "You know a dog named Carlos?"

"The lady next door owned him. He had a blue eye and his tail got caught in a car door," she said, smelling her hand. "Your head stinks," she added.

"It's my brain."

"What's wrong with it?"

"It's rotting away," I said, half-serious. "That's why I gotta keep my head shaved."

She said, "Don't sucker me, sucker."

I could see into one of her ears. It was full of brown wax. She really was dirty. I felt pretty sorry for her. And just as I was about to give her this little hug, she

127

reached over and grabbed my pepper shaker and blackened her tongue with it.

"You like pepper?" I asked.

"Kills germs," she said. "Bugs and blackteria and stuff."

"*Bac*teria," I said, correcting her.

"Bacteria, blackteria, same difference. Makes you burp, too."

She swallowed and then showed me her tongue, which had returned to its original pink.

Then she said, "Hey, you wanna have a burping contest?"

"Not really," I said.

"Too chicken, huh?"

"I'm not very good at it."

Which was true. Dantly can burp so loud, it sounds like a Harley. I've never been able to do it, though, which is probably a good thing.

The girl went, "I can out-burp every kid who comes in here." She made this face like she was being filled with some great, unspoken holy knowledge, then she swallowed a gulp of air and burped impressively.

I was like, "Not bad."

"Anytime you're ready to go head-to-head, just let me know."

I was suddenly starving for a cigarette. I could have

eaten one, I swear, but the Foote no-smoking laws had been instated only a month before and I would have been kicked out.

When I looked up, the girl was eyeing my bag.

"Why you runnin' away?" she asked.

I was like, "I'm not."

"I ain't stupid," she said. "What's your name, anyway?" she asked.

I said, "Nitro," just to mess with her.

"*Nitro,*" she said. "Nitro *Chickenhead*. It's prolly like *Dave* or somethin'."

"It's Steve," I said.

"Lemme have some fries, Steve," she said, grabbing a handful. She totally chewed with her mouth open.

I looked over at the heavyset guy. He was eating a huge slice of apple pie now. He was pretty pleased about it, too.

"What's your name?" I asked the girl.

"June."

"June what?"

"Just June." Then she slid into my booth and said, "Knock, knock," reaching across the table for my ginger ale, making it hers, and guzzling it down in a very impressive three-part move.

"Who's there?" I said.

"Yougot."

"Yougot who?"

"You got blue paint all over your shirt. Knock, knock," she said again.

"Who's there?"

"Orange."

"Orange who?"

"Oranja glad I didn't pinchya in the arm?"

"Good one."

She shifted in the seat a bit and said, "You got a girlfriend?"

"No" I said, checking out the front of my shirt, which had blue paint all over it.

"That's too bad. You're cute."

"Thanks," I said, realizing that she'd just finished all my fries. I managed to get my ginger ale back from her and took a gulp. She was a total con artist, this girl.

"Hey," I said, "is someone like watching you?"

"No."

"Why not?"

"I don't need nobody to watch me."

"Do you like have parents?" I asked.

"I got a mom."

"Where is she?"

"Workin'."

"Does she know where you are?"

"Yeah. She picks me up every day here."

"What's she do?" I asked.

"She's a professional dancer."

"Like a *dancer* dancer?"

"Like for videos. Ballerinas and stuff. Can I get some more pop?"

I let June have the rest of my ginger ale. She drank it and then started chewing my ice.

Then the waitress came over with a pot of coffee and dropped my check.

"Don't let this one bamboozle you," she said, and turned and limped to the other side of the diner, where she poured coffee for the elderly lady who was reading the paperback.

June chewed some more ice and went, "So you wanna go to the movies with me?"

I said, "Like the *movies* movies?"

"Yeah, like *Star Trek* and *Forrest Glum* and stuff."

"What about your mom?"

"What about her?"

"Isn't she coming to pick you up?"

"Oh, she don't come till later."

"I don't have much money," I said.

It was rude of me to lie to a little girl, I admit, but I had to start thinking long-term. At this point I had no idea where I was going to spend the night. I figured if nothing came along, I could get a room at the YMCA.

"I got money," June said, producing a crinkled one-hundred-dollar bill from some secret fold in her pickle shirt. She smoothed it on the table. Ben Franklin looked like he'd just gotten his hair done. It was totally wavy like a woman's.

I left five bucks on the table and grabbed my bag.

Before we left, June ran into the bathroom.

The heavyset guy was guzzling ice water now and the waitress was setting another piece of apple pie in front of him. Man, that guy could put it away.

A moment later, June returned from the bathroom with a roll of toilet paper. "In case we cry," she said, handing it to me. I stuffed it into my bag and she took my hand.

As we were leaving, the elderly lady with the sad gray eyes started laughing into her book. Something was so funny she could have died right there and gone to heaven. It was weird, though, because she had this totally ugly, over-the-top man's laugh. I could practically feel it crawling on my skin.

June took me to this movie about a crippled boy who finds a magic horse in the field behind his family's farmhouse. The kid has to use these metal crutches to walk, and it's obvious that you're supposed to start feeling totally sorry for him in the first scene when he tries to kick a half-deflated tetherball and falls flat on his face in a pile of pig feces.

We tried to get into the spy movie with the Scottish guy in the Lamborghini, but the girl at the counter wouldn't sell the tickets to us because it was rated NC-17.

June bought a big tub of popcorn and fell asleep on my shoulder about ten minutes after the opening credits.

During the movie, I kept thinking about the blue wall and my dad and my mom dying and Welton and how totally screwed up everything was over in East Foote. For some reason I started crying. I can cry pretty well without any sound. It gets all trapped in my throat and it makes me feel like my face is going to burst, but it's a good technique, especially when there's a little kid sleeping on your shoulder. I removed June's toilet paper from my bag. I probably used half the roll wiping my face.

After the movie, I shook June, who was still like totally snoring on my shoulder. There was a little pool of saliva on the sleeve of my squirrel-with-human-testicles T-shirt.

"Rise and shine," I said.

June nodded and got up and walked up the aisle like I wasn't even there. For a second I thought she might have been sleepwalking, so I followed her out. First she got a drink from the water fountain and then she turned this circle all sleepy and disoriented and went into the women's bathroom.

In the lobby there were all these families buying popcorn and candy. This one little kid with a Sammy Sosa T-shirt kept begging his dad for a quarter. He wanted to play this awesome deer-hunting game called Big Buck Hunter II, but his dad kept ignoring him and going on and on to a friend about the stock market and how much money he was going to make on some new dot-com company.

"Post-crash and everything," he kept saying. "Who would've thought? A dot-commer."

The little kid had a crewcut and huge ears. You could totally tell that his dad made him get the crewcut, too, like he was being groomed for the Marines or whatever. The kid had that kind of blond hair that looks almost white. He tugged at his dad's belt about three more times but he couldn't get his attention, so I yelled at him.

I said, "Give the kid a quarter!"

Man, I never do stuff like that. It just sort of blurted out of me. That's how you get into fistfights, and I'm definitely not a fighter.

The kid's dad stopped talking to his friend and just sort of stared at me. His eyes were hard and little, like they had been drilled into his skull with a screw gun. He looked like so many of the other dads in Foote. Magazine hair. Clothes the color of ice cream. Shoes from that men's store in the mall. The perfect white teeth. It was like some artist had *sculpted* them or whatever.

"Why don't you mind your own frigging business, smart guy," the kid's dad said. He was short, but he had one of those necks. Like he was captain of the rugby team or something. His crewcut went thin at the top of his head. He was probably one of those totally senseless guys who head-butts the refrigerator on a daily basis.

His wife put her hand on his shoulder, but he

brushed it off all macho-like. Then she put it back on and said something that they say on TV when a woman's trying to stop her husband from fighting.

That's when I gave him the finger, which surprised *me* even, and he made a quick move toward me, but his Internet friend practically jumped on his back, and then his wife dropped this big tub of popcorn and it was suddenly everywhere.

I stood there and glared at Dad in his Dockers and his nice plaid summer shirt and his mahogany tan and his cell phone stuck to the side of his belt like some kind of electric black bug that he couldn't get rid of. The bald spot on the top of his head was so red it looked like it would pop. He was leering at me like he wanted to slaughter me and feed me to his family.

"Easy, Jack. Easy now, buddy, it's not worth it," the Internet friend said to him. Then to me he said, "Nice shirt. Real mature."

The guy behind the refreshments counter offered the wife another tub of popcorn, and she nodded and thanked him and told him how sweet he was.

"Don't even look at the freak," the Internet friend told the kid's dad. "Don't even look at him."

Then the kid's dad got himself together and brushed off his pants and pinched the creases.

It had been about ten minutes since June disappeared into the women's bathroom. I was starting to worry. I was tempted to go in after her, but all these elderly women kept staring me down. They had just come out from that sequel about the senior citizens who get sucked up into a spaceship.

"What's in the bag?" the kid's dad shouted at me. "A *bomb*?"

Then this manager with a clip-on tie finally came out to calm the crowd. The guy looked more like an undertaker than someone who ran a multiplex movie theater. He was really tall—way taller than me, maybe like six nine or something—and he slouched so badly I thought he had some sort of medical condition.

The kid's dad explained the situation to the manager, and he and his wife and his friend pointed at me several times, and the manager nodded and apologized for my behavior and offered them a bunch of free tickets, which they accepted with hearty handshakes. After that, the movie manager guy took a few steps toward me and pointed.

"Move along now, friend," he said.

"I'm waiting for someone," I explained.

"Who exactly are you waiting for?"

"My little sister," I said. "She's in the bathroom."

"This is a public theater, where everyone deserves to seek out entertainment in peace," he said. He was obviously doing everything he was supposed to under the circumstances.

For some reason, his speech made me want to sit right on the water fountain, so that's what I did.

"Hey, now!" the manager cried. "You can't sit on that!"

Fortunately June came out or I'm sure he would've called the cops. She still looked sort of dazed, and she was holding a new roll of toilet paper.

"Hey," she said.

"Hey," I said. "You okay?"

"This old lady wouldn't come out of the crapper. She was like changing her wig and stuff."

"Let's get out of here," I said.

June took my hand, and we walked toward the glass doors. Just as we passed that family, I removed a quarter from my pocket and tossed it to the little kid. He caught it and turned it in his hand.

"Give me that!" his dad demanded, and the kid handed him the quarter.

That guy hated me so much it was making him crazy. I had ruined his afternoon, and I must admit that I was glad. Later that evening, at home, he would punch a hole in the wall in the bedroom—I could just see it. Then all of their wedding pictures would fall off the dresser. And after that he and his Internet friend would come searching for me in his Ford Explorer. The thought made me paranoid and itchy.

Outside, the heat was on us like an animal.

"You missed a good movie," I told June.

"I watched it," she said. "It was about a dog, right?"

We headed back toward the diner.

"Hey, lemme have a cigarette," June said as we crossed the street. She could obviously see my Camel Lights sticking out of my back pocket.

I said, "You're way too young to smoke."

She said, "So are you."

Which was true at that point.

"I don't even inhale," she said. "C'mon, Steve, lemme have one."

We stopped at the McDonald's and sat at one of the picnic tables. Someone had overturned a Dumpster, and trash was everywhere. I handed June a Camel Light and lit it for her. And then I lit one for myself.

Man, most little kids smoke like their eyeballs itch, but June smoked like a film star. She would take these long drags and everything.

The streetlamps were starting to go on everywhere, and you could see moths and mosquitoes swirling.

"Hey, Steve," June said. "What were you cryin' about, anyway?"

I said, "What?"

"During the movie," she said.

"I wasn't crying."

"Yes, you was. The movie wasn't *that* good."

"Finish your cigarette and I'll walk you back to the diner."

We smoked and watched the trash whip around for a few minutes. Trash will make some pretty interesting shapes if you watch it long enough. I thought maybe it was trying to tell me something. Like my future or whatever.

We walked back to the diner and stood outside waiting for her mom, who I wasn't yet sure really existed. The heat was making things slide down the sides of buildings. It was like Foote was totally sweating or something.

Through the window of the diner, I could see the same waitress from before. She was carrying a full pot of coffee. She never actually poured it; she just sort of wandered around aimlessly with it, like some battery-powered Christmas toy.

"What are you doing tomorrow?" June asked.

"I'm not sure," I said. "Why?"

"You should come by. We could go see another movie. The one about those aliens."

Just then this dark blue, totally lopsided Pinto pulled up in front of the diner. The windows were smoked ghetto-style, and you could see the streetlights sort of trapped in glass like bewildered fireflies.

"Let's go, June-June!" a woman shouted from the driver's side.

"Later," June said, snapping twice, pinching the back of my arm as hard as she could, and then turning and running toward the car in another impressive multipart move. Man, this kid had more moves than those white R&B guys with all the music videos.

June got in and closed the door, and then the Pinto pulled off down the street, a cloud of silver exhaust sort of coughing out the back. The back license plate was missing, and although I know that's illegal, I was just relieved to see that someone actually did come and pick June up.

After the Pinto disappeared, I looked through the window of Jack Palomino's again. The waitress had set the pot of coffee down on a table, where it was burning through the linoleum. It would leave a black ring, but I supposed no one would mind much.

That old woman was still in there, reading the same paperback. She never slept, I thought; she just constantly read. Or maybe she was faking it the whole time. Maybe she never actually read a single word.

For some reason I had this fear that she was going to get locked in with that depressing waitress, and I wanted to bang on the window and scream at her to leave, but I didn't. Instead, I turned and headed down the street.

It was that hour when everything starts to look not quite real. The trees. The parked cars. All the windows on the office buildings. It's like someone drew it all on the back of a racing form or something.

I didn't even know what direction I was heading. All I knew was that the sun was setting pretty quickly and I wanted to get somewhere before it was totally dark.

Later it started to pour.

You're probably thinking, *Of course it poured,* right? Well, I'm not simply trying to be dramatic — it really did pour, I swear.

And it started about three blocks before I got to the YMCA, so I was pretty much soaked by the time I got there.

In downtown Foote there's the old Y and the new Y. The new Y is this totally blond-brick building with a big, overly lit, multicolored YMCA sign. It has one of those million-dollar Olympic pools and a yoga room and video games in the lobby and modern vending machines with ergonomic punch pads. It probably has like some totally user-friendly community e-mail room too.

From the parking lot, the old Y looks like some failed arsonist's project. The limestone is stained and the windows are sooty black and the entrance looks totally untrustworthy and somehow rigged, like there's a trapdoor just beyond the threshold. The building hogs an entire block, and it pretty much comes across as being either totally haunted or condemned.

On the inside, the old Y feels like some strange cross between a mental institution and a halfway house for war criminals. In the main room there's a small collection of lopsided bumper-pool tables whose half-upholstered surfaces are choked with ashtrays and racing forms. Slashed and maimed chairs are randomly arranged among the bumper-pool tables like some weird furniture virus. Beached on these pathetic furnishings is a species of man not known to most. They are male, yes. They are vaguely conscious, yes. They are also semi-overweight, incredibly suspicious-looking hairy guys either half watching TV with the sound turned up too high or playing an endless game of poker. And most of them have at least one hand stuffed down their pants. They live in this room the way certain creatures inhabit square footage at the zoo.

Once Welton told me that people don't go swimming at the old Y; these ageless freaks just take turns defecating in the pool.

It's only like twelve bucks to stay the night, which worked perfectly well with my meager budget. When I asked for a room, the guy behind the desk studied me for about ten minutes before he spoke. I thought he was either deaf or stoned out of his mind. His teeth were the color of the parking lot.

I told him I got locked out of my house and that my parents were out of town. He nodded through most of it, and then when he finally gave me a key, his lips parted and for some reason he smiled this huge smile that revealed other fantastic mysteries of his mouth. For instance, there was this totally cancerous-looking black spot in the center of his tongue. I'd seen German shepherds with better mouths.

The towel he pushed toward me looked like something you'd use to wipe off a toilet seat. It was probably infested with VD. I gave him a twenty, and he pushed eight bucks back at me like it was something I had to eat.

"Clear out by eleven," he instructed. "If you want the room another night, you gotta pay up by noon. Don't use the machines on the fourth floor 'cause they'll eat your money. And you gotta let the showers run for a minute before the hot water kicks in. And the elevator's currently being serviced, so you gotta use the stairs."

He rapped his knuckles on the desk a few times and added, "And no smoking in the room. If you wanna smoke, go to the corner lounge. Or come down here. You smoke?" he asked.

I was like, "Yeah, why?"

"Can I get a cigarette?"

145

I reached into my dad's bag and produced a half-empty pack of Camel Lights. He took two and winked at me.

"I'll get you back," he said. He had already lit a match and started smoking by the time I turned and headed for the stairs.

My room was on the sixth floor.

Man, the stairwell smelled terrible. And it wasn't exactly what you'd call well lit. Each time I got to a new floor, I felt like someone was going to like totally jump out and get all kung fu on me.

The room I got is best described as being a glorified closet. It was like four times worse than what they give you here at Burnstone Grove. The twin bed looked like some little kid had died in it. It was made up with these totally sad, urine-yellow sheets, a moth-eaten comforter, and a pillow that was about as fluffy as a folded dishrag. The mattress was lumpy and smelled like pets and weather.

Also featured in my twelve-dollar room were a metal desk-slash-dresser ensemble, a sink complete with rusty faucet and cracked mirror, and a small, overly painted closet door that I was afraid to open.

The room's only saving grace was a naked window overlooking the back alley and an iron fire escape slanting across the pane. Man, there's something about fire escapes that I love. I can totally gaze at them all day. Maybe it's because they're sort of like these secret places where you can just sit and smoke and think.

One summer when we were kids, my mom took me and Welton down to Sullivan, Illinois, to visit our aunt Ricky. Before she married Uncle Mike and moved to Iowa, Aunt Ricky lived in this old apartment building in southern Illinois that had this amazing fire escape. Welton and I were like eleven and ten then. We spent that entire Saturday watching cars and spitting, our legs hanging over the edge of the fire escape. My mom was cool and brought our dinners out to us and let us eat right there out on the fire escape. Later on, it started raining and all the pedestrians pulled out umbrellas and they sort of bloomed like these giant flowers. And the rain had turned the streets shiny and the cars looked like toys and it was a beautiful moment in my life.

Welton even captured it in that weird way of his. He went, "Black roses, Steve. Look at all those black roses."

In the alley below the window of my room at the old Y, there was a man sitting against a brick wall. The rain had stopped, but he was soaked. He kept clawing at his chest and arms. He was probably being devoured by mosquitoes. Either that or he was just sick of it all. It was like he was trying to claw his skin off so he could start over or something.

I couldn't tell if he was homeless or just trying to hide. I watched him for about five minutes and decided that he wasn't either. He was just there. This was his place in the world. One person gets a corner office in a big city overlooking the ticker-tape parade, and someone else gets a urine-stained wall in the back alley of downtown Foote, Iowa. It all comes down to destiny or irony or one of those things you're supposed to learn about in English class. *Dentistry or Ironing* I saw written on one of Welton's English Lit notebooks.

Above the desk there was this framed picture of Jesus. He was reaching his hand out and making this face like he was about to get shot. I couldn't stand looking at it—it reminded me of the Jesus picture back in my room at home. I tried to take it down, but it was bolted into the wall, so I wound up stripping my pillowcase and draping it over the frame.

After that I unlaced my Red Wing boots and let my feet breathe. I know I wasn't doing much for the general smell of the room, but I didn't care.

There were voices in the next room. Two men and a woman. It sounded like they were playing hearts because of the way one of the men kept saying how the woman was trying to shoot the moon. Her name was Georgia and she had a voice like a clarinet.

I have to admit, for a second it was sort of turning me on, because I kept imagining Georgia in a very positive light. She was donning designer swimwear with fringe or whatever and she was lying on her stomach with the bikini-top straps untied. I was lathering her up with sunblock and my hands were getting into all the cracks and crevices. The image got me pretty excited, and before I knew it, I had an erection. At first I thought it would go away, but it kept getting worse, like harder in that painful way. So that's when I did something a little weird—I started barking at it. Like a Great Dane or a pit bull or whatever. I literally barked at my erection!

And it worked, I'm not kidding.

"Ruff!" I barked at my erection. "Ruff, ruff!"

When things finally calmed down, I stretched out in the bed and tried to let my head go blank.

Bur Georgia was sort of laughing again.

"She's shooting the moon!" one of the men shouted. "She's doing it *again*! She's shooting the fucking *moon,* bro!"

Man, my head was starting to totally spin. I got out of bed and walked about fifty circles to try to catch up to it. I thought I was going to faint, so I grabbed a pack of Camel Lights and a bottle of Robitussin out of my dad's Marine Corps bag and practically ran out of the room.

The hall was empty and brown, and it smelled like that sawdust the janitor uses at the gifted school when some kid vomits in the room with all the xylophones. There was a sign taped to the wall with an arrow pointing to the end of the hall. It said SMORKING. I'm not trying to be cocky or anything, but I'd bet some free cell phone minutes that it was supposed to say SMOKING. Not to get philosophical or anything, but I think there's like *one guy* who puts up all those signs. THIS WAY. SMOKING. PLEASE REMOVE SHOES. NO PARKING ANY TIME. DON'T LOOK DOWN. He probably like lives under the city and all he does is watch TV reruns until those color bands come on the screen and then he climbs up from under some sub-basement at like five A.M. or whatever and pastes those signs up in the blue-black light of the early morning.

Once I heard Dantly tell Welton that the Native Americans used to call that particular part of the morning "between the wolf and the dog" because the sky is so deep blue and spooky or whatever that you can't tell what's what. Is that a wolf on that hill or a dog? A man or a monkey? A saint or the devil?

The floor was cold and clammy against my bare feet. It felt like I was walking in some random hospital where a bunch of toilets had overflowed into the hall. I had that weird rust sensation in my mouth again, and I could taste the diner hot dog crawling up the back of my throat. Man, I totally thought I was going to puke, but I managed to keep it together.

In the lounge there were about eight overstuffed chairs and a few coffee tables and so many ashtrays you would have thought that they had arrived there first and the furniture was brought in just to make things fair.

This priest was reading next to the window. In the lamplight he looked pretty lost and lonely. He was holding a lit cigarette and the smoke was curling into the bottom of the lampshade, all slow and moody. Even though he didn't appear to be a very big guy, he had maybe the longest fingers I've ever seen.

I sat down in a chair that smelled like alcohol and potting soil. I tapped out a cigarette and lit it. The priest was making this totally unreadable expression. I couldn't tell if he was happy or sad. He was wearing a pair of glasses that it made it sort of difficult to make out his eyes.

I opened my Robitussin and took a drink.

"Are you okay?" the priest asked. His voice was

clean and friendly. He had dipped his glasses down on the tip of his nose so he could see me. He was a lot younger than I thought, probably in his thirties.

I said, "I'm okay. Why?"

"You're drinking cold medicine."

He pushed his glasses back on the bridge of his nose.

"Summer flu," I said, screwing the top back on the bottle.

The priest closed his book. It was *The Power and the Glory* by Someone Greene.

He stared at me for a moment.

"Are you from town here?" he asked.

"Yes," I said. "East Foote, actually."

Then he smoked and exhaled and crossed his legs. His cigarette was burning so slow I was starting to think that he made some cheap deal with the tobacco devil.

"Is everything okay at home?" he asked.

"Yeah," I said. "Everything's fine, why?"

"Well, you're spending the night at the Y."

I could totally see what he was talking about. I must have been pretty suspicious-looking.

"How old are you, if you don't mind me asking?"

"Eighteen," I said, lying.

"Do you go to Governors?"

"I go to the gifted school. In East Foote."

"I see," he said.

After a minute, to change the subject, I went, "Are you like a priest?"

He was like, "Yes, I am actually. I am indeed a priest."

"What religion?"

"Roman Catholic."

For some reason I blessed him. I was like, "God bless you."

"Well, thank you," he said.

God, I've never been such a smart-ass. I have no idea what got into me. But that was just the beginning.

I said, "No. I mean it, man. God bless you and your family."

"Well, I don't actually have a family," he explained. "In layperson's terms, that is. In a figurative way, my parish is my family."

I then said, "Well, God bless your figure, then."

The priest chuckled a few times and said, "Are you Catholic?"

"I was raised Catholic, but that ended."

"When did that end?"

"I don't know," I said. "I guess when Christmases started sucking."

He laughed again and smoked.

"What parish did your family attend?"

"St. Rose's over in East Foote."

"Of course," he said. "Father Newman's an old friend."

I unscrewed the top of my Robitussin and took another drink. I could feel the syrupy warmth starting to swell in my chest.

Our conversation stopped for a minute. I smoked about half of my Camel Light and he stared out the window. You could see that it had started to rain again.

After a minute the priest rose out of his chair and came toward me with his hand extended. For a split second I thought he was going to like bless me to death or something, but all he wanted was a handshake. The guy was like six inches shorter than me, but he made me feel totally nervous.

"I'm Father Bob," he said. "Father Bob Underwood. What's your name?"

"June," I said.

"June," he repeated.

"Yeah, June," I said. "June Nugent."

"Well, it's nice to meet you, June," he said, taking his hand back and returning to his chair by the window.

We sat in silence again. Our cigarette smoke was making these totally weird, ghostly shapes. For some reason I was starting to get really nervous.

After a moment I said, "So, Father Bob, can I ask you a question?"

He replied, "Of course."

I had no idea what was going to come out of my mouth — I really didn't.

"What's like your take on God?"

"I'm not sure I understand the gist of your question, June."

"I mean, like the big bang and all that. The holy mysteries. Like what's his plan?"

"His plan?"

"Yeah, his plan."

"Well, June, I would say his plan is love."

"But what does that actually *mean*?" I asked.

"It means that he wants us to spread love. To help each other. Have you ever heard of the golden rule?"

"Yeah," I said. "But that just seems sort of fake to me."

"I'm afraid it's not, though. It's not fake at all. Sometimes it's just a matter of simply letting Him in."

"Father Bob," I heard myself saying, "what I guess I'm asking is, if God is this holy *force* or whatever, then where is he? Does he hang out at the mall? Is he like hiding under some holy log in Jerusalem?"

"God is everywhere, June."

"But what does that *mean?* Is he like a tree or—or—or—or like a *bird?* I mean, is he like *oxygen?*"

"In a manner of speaking, yes, June, he very much *is* oxygen."

"And how do you like get the guy to help you? How do you get *oxygen* to take some interest?"

"Well, you pray."

"But I used to pray all the time, and he never came through. For instance, I'd be at the dog track. And I'd be down to my last two dollars, and I'd like put my hands together and totally look up at the sky and ask God to let the four dog come in the top two so I could win the quinella."

"Well, June, one shouldn't use prayer as a means to *obtain* things. That's not what God intended."

"I'll tell you something, Father Bob. Nine times out of ten, the four dog *doesn't* finish in the top two. Nine times out of *ten.* And like my mother . . ."

I had to stop because I was suddenly hyperventilating like crazy.

"What *about* your mother, June?"

I tried taking a drag on my cigarette, but I dropped it on the floor and accidentally stomped it out. I couldn't even light another one because my hands were shaking so bad. About four others fell on the floor and

156

rolled under this totally diseased-looking half-sofa. I practically wasted an entire pack of Camel Lights.

"June," Father Bob said, "is your mother okay?"

Suddenly I was coughing so bad it was like I had lung cancer. I coughed about forty-seven times.

Father Bob was suddenly pointing at my face.

I said, "Why are you pointing at me?"

"Your nose is bleeding."

I touched my nose and then looked at my fingers. There was so much blood it was like I had been shot.

Father Bob then rose out of his chair again and produced a white handkerchief and was starting to ease it toward my face when I swiped his hand away.

I was like, "Don't!"

There was blood all down the front of my shirt now.

"Okay," Father Bob said, taking the handkerchief back. "I'm just trying to help."

"I mean, what are you *doing* here, anyway?" I said.

Father Bob said, "I live here, June."

"You *live* here?"

"There was a fire at the rectory last week. It's just temporary."

"Stay away from me!" I practically screamed.

"I'm not coming near you, June," Father Bob said, all calm and collected. "I was just trying to help you."

That's when I stood.

Man, I was suddenly so wasted I could hardly keep my balance. I pushed past all the orphaned furniture and zigzagged back down the hall. The walls were so brown, it was like someone had smeared them with feces.

As soon as I got back to my room, I locked the door and lurched to the sink. In the cracked mirror, my reflection was this total horror movie. I had no hair, and about a gallon of blood was gushing from my nose.

I'd started to wash my face when there was a knock on my door.

"June?" I heard.

It was Father Bob.

"June, are you okay?"

I turned the water off.

I imagined him leaning up against the door, all lonely and sad, with his weird long fingers sort of touching the door.

"June," he said, "you left your cold medicine in the lounge."

I said, "Keep it."

"Why don't you open the door?"

"No," I said. "Leave me alone."

"I don't want to hurt you, June. No one wants to hurt you."

I didn't answer. I could see his feet under the crack in the door. We were quiet for a minute. All I could hear was my own breathing.

"Okay, then. I'm just going to leave your medicine in the hall. It'll be right here on the other side."

After a minute his feet disappeared and I could hear his footsteps fading down the hall. I didn't open the door for the rest of the night. I wouldn't have opened that door if someone had held a gun to my head.

The first thing I did after Father Bob walked off was I got cleaned up in the sink. My nose finally stopped bleeding, but it took me about a half an hour to get all the blood off my face. Man, blood is by far the hardest thing to clean off your skin.

After I got cleaned up, I did about the dumbest thing I've ever done—I went into the closet. Not even an hour before, you couldn't have paid me a million dollars to open that closet, but I suddenly decided it would be okay, so I went inside and closed the door. The reason it was so stupid is because I sort of pretended like it was a telephone booth, and I called Welton. I like totally dropped a quarter in the coin slot and everything.

Welton said, "Hello?"

And I said, "Hey, Welton. It's Steve."

"Hey, bro."

"What's goin on?" I said.

He said, "Nothin', dude. Where are you?"

I said, "I'm at the Y, man."

He went, "Like the *Y* Y?"

"Yeah," I said. "The one in Foote. The old one with all the bumper-pool tables."

He said, "The old Y?"

And I was so cool—I really was. I said, "Yeah, man. The *old* Y. Nothing but weirdos here."

Then Welton said, "So why are you calling, bro?"

"Well," I replied, "you remember that summer when Mom took us down to southern Illinois to visit Aunt Ricky and we like sat on the fire escape?"

Welton was like, "Yeah, bro. I *totally* remember that."

"And how we were dangling our legs and target-spitting and then Mom like brought root beers and sloppy joes out to us and then it started raining and all those umbrellas came out. How they like *bloomed*?"

"Yeah, bro. They totally *bloomed*."

"They were like black roses, weren't they?"

Welton said, "They were *totally* like black roses."

"That was the best, wasn't it?"

"That was the best, bro."

"It was *so* the best. . . ."

That's when the phone conversation ended. I can't remember who hung up first. All I know is that I was standing in the closet and my mouth was so dry it was like I had eaten sand. I tried to swallow, but the walls of my throat kept sticking together. I sat down on the floor and started to sing this Bottomside song called "Forty Holes and Forty Goals" that Welton always listened to. I only knew this one part of the song, but I sang it over and over.

there's a hole
in my head
there's a hole
in my pocket
there's a hole
in the floor
there's a hole
in the door
i'm gonna find it
i'm gonna fill it
there's a hole

I sang that part of the song over and over. And my mouth was so dry and my throat was so raw and tired, but I kept singing it.

After about a while—it might have been an hour,

no kidding—I stopped singing and came out of the closet and went to the sink and slurped water out of my hand for like ten minutes straight.

Then I crossed to the window and looked down at the alley. It was still raining, and there was some wet cardboard where that guy from before had been sitting. Someone probably came by and stabbed him to death and dragged him into the river. Someone from one of those Caucasian rap-video gangs. They either stabbed him or strangled him with pantyhose.

I eventually made my way to the bed. I stared up at the ceiling for a while and fell asleep wondering how I was going to get through the next few days.

18

"So, your dad's coming to see you next week," Mrs. Leene said, starting out our session today.

She was wearing this green turtleneck sweater that accentuated her breasts nicely, but I have to admit that since I made out with Silent Starla, I've been less attracted to Mrs. Leene.

"Are you looking forward to seeing him?" she asked.

"I don't know," I said. "Maybe."

"I had a good talk with him. I think he's in a better place. The counseling has really helped him."

She was talking about this guy from the Veterans Hospital in Davenport who my dad was seeing once a week. I guess he is half–grief counselor, half–military counselor.

"The visit might be really good for you two. Maybe it's time."

After my session, I had lunch with Silent Starla. We watched each other eat and smiled a lot. She kept sort of playing with my foot under the table, and I couldn't stop blushing, which is a problem I can't control.

"You're blushing again," she teased me, still playing with my foot.

What's weird is that it only happens in one of my cheeks, like the other one is more sophisticated or something.

"You're so pretty," I had said to her earlier.

"Don't lie," she said back.

"I'm not lying."

"Eat your food," she said. But she was smiling when she said it, so I know she liked my compliment.

But I don't want to get too sidetracked about Silent Starla and how pretty she is.

Back to the story part.

So the morning after my night at the old Y, I was walking up the hill on Governors Boulevard. It was maybe ten-thirty and already boiling hot.

These three jocks with shaved heads were mowing the Governors College baseball field. They all had washboard abs and these totally perfect, Coppertone-tan chests, and you could tell they knew how all the cars were slowing down to watch them.

My eyes were raw and my stitches were burning pretty bad. I was starting to worry about my shin being infected—like things turning green or whatever—

when the Skylark pulled in front of me. There was a familiar bumper sticker above the license plate: WWW.FUCKYOU.COM.

It was Dantly.

The Skylark idled on the side of the road like a beast waiting for food. There was so much exhaust spilling everywhere, it was as if the car had been damned to carry a little part of hell with it wherever it went.

Dantly's head sort of lolled out the open window, his greasy, brown, unintentionally half-dreadlocked hair spilling down the driver's-side door. During the small amount of time between pulling over and putting the car in park, I think he might have actually fallen asleep. It was the dreamless sleep of a cow or a fish.

No one's ever really known how old Dantly actually is. He might be nineteen, but he could also be like thirty-seven, too. Once I asked Welton.

"He's as old as you want him to be," my brother responded.

No one knows where Dantly lives, either. He just sort of *appears* places, like Santa Claus or the Easter Bunny. It's like *poof* and there he is, driving his souped-up Skylark.

And Welton used to swear that Dantly has like eighteen tattoos. Once he apparently drove all the way to Kansas City because he heard about this tattoo artist who would drop acid and draw his visions on the small of your back. I've never seen Dantly's tattoos, but the lore is that his back is filled with pythons and bulls playing badminton in plaid pajamas and flying mermaids and other things of this nature. I've asked him to show me a bunch of times, but he always says he would have to charge me ten bucks.

There's definitely something semi-supernatural about the guy. He's never worked out or played sports but he's more cut than most jocks. I think it's because of all those hard-core drugs he does. Somehow they've had a reverse effect on him and actually *developed* his muscles.

"Steve Nugent, is that you, kid?" he shouted over the engine. His voice was hoarse with the night before. Or maybe it was permanently damaged now.

He said, "What's up, bra?"

I answered, "Not much," and approached the Skylark carefully.

Up close you could see how totally wasted he was. His mouth was half-open like someone had just kicked him in the neck. His tongue seemed too heavy for his mouth. His facial hair was all random and extra-long in places. His pupils were so dilated, they were like the eyes of a stuffed animal.

"Dude," he said, "what happened to your hair?"

"I shaved it off," I answered, palming my skull with my free hand.

"Bald for the new millennium," he said, lighting a cigarette out of nowhere, somehow making spontaneous fire with his fingers. I think that's one of those things that just starts happening after you've smoked enough illegal substances—your body starts producing small flames.

Dantly snorted and said, "Where you walkin' to?"

"Over to Carroll to register for a class."

He sang, *"Summer school,"* evilly, like it had been something that either brought him great joy or great disgust. Man, I couldn't even picture Dantly in a high school *parking lot,* let alone a classroom.

He coughed and swallowed phlegm. "Hop in."

Getting in the Skylark was like stepping into a canoe full of water moccasins.

Man, his car really stank. It was one of those personal smells, like an uncle's room, but multiplied by fifty. The back seat was full of so much half-eaten fast food, I was surprised there weren't small animals scurrying around.

Dantly pulled away from the curb and dug something black out of his nose. I think it was some sort of a bug. He flicked it blindly into the back seat and went,

"I thought you were supposed to be some kinda *genius,* man. What class did you blow off?"

I was like, "I didn't. The gifted school said I could graduate early if I took a creative writing class."

"That's right," Dantly sneered. "You go to the *gifted school.*" He smoked and exhaled. His teeth were sort of blue and they seemed too short.

We approached a red light, and for a second I wasn't sure if he was going to actually stop, but he did at the last second. I almost hit my head on the dashboard, but Dantly made an arm bar to stop me, thank God.

"Just keeping you on yer toes," he said, and snorted again.

Suddenly something smelled like it was burning.

I said, "Dantly, do you smell that?"

He said, "What, did you fart or somethin'?"

"No," I said, "something's burning."

"Oh. That's just the radiator. Nothing to be alarmed about."

Then Dantly turned on the radio to a seventies rock song. Some white dude on acid was murdering his guitar.

In the passenger-side mirror, I could still see those three jocks who'd been mowing the baseball field.

They were playing Frisbee now and had shrunk down to the size of fleas.

While we waited for the light to change, Dantly said, "Creative writing in July. Then what—college?"

I said, "I don't know. Probably."

"Corporate America, here you come! Rock on, young Nugent!"

I said, "Rock on. Right."

The light turned green, and he gunned the Skylark for a few seconds, then slowed down. For a few blocks we drove in that weird silence that thickens between two people who don't really know each other.

For some reason Dantly suddenly started punching the steering wheel—literally punching it like it was a kid he'd forgotten to beat up back in the eighties. We almost swerved into a little girl riding a mountain bike. Her bike was so big, it made her seem all weird and inanimate, like she was a doll. When I looked back, she had stopped riding.

Then for some reason Dantly said, "Jesus and Santa Claus got caught stealing shit at the mall last week. Get it?"

"Sure," I said.

I actually didn't get it at all and I still don't. But he thought it was funny.

In the rearview mirror I could see that that little girl was walking the bike now, and she had to use every muscle in her body to keep it from falling over.

Dantly swerved back to the center of the street and went, "Someday you're prolly gonna wind up like running a fucking Starbucks or some shit."

I was like, "Doubt it."

"Start starchin' your collars. Press those trouserly trousers, my lanky East Foote brother. The days of dry cleaning and Chinese takeout are just around the corner."

I didn't say anything.

More smells from the back seat were starting to form.

"Dude," Dantly said. "You should like go into the *army.*"

"I don't think so," I responded.

"Seriously, though," Dantly continued, "think about that shit. They got *chicks* in the army now. *Clean* chicks. Babes in unis, man."

"Yeah, babes in unis," I echoed.

"Plus you get to travel around. Drive tanks. Sail the seven seas. Be all you can be and all that. Get the fuck outta this place."

"Maybe."

"I hear shooting an M-16 gives you a boner."

I said, "Cool."

The song with the guitar murder ended, and now they were running a commercial about some car with rack-and-pinion steering. How it would like totally save your life with no money down. The guy speaking sounded like he was on coke.

"What," Dantly said, "you wanna wind up like *me*? Me or your dipshit *brother*? I mean, look at us, kid."

I looked at him, and he totally had a point. I think one of his eyes was permanently closed.

"Oh, by the way," he said suddenly, "sorry about the old bird, man. Mary Lee Nugent was a cool lady. Welton said the funeral was a trip. Everyone cryin' and shit. Nothing like a roomful of bawling relatives. Fucking family, man . . ."

We turned onto Vista Street. College buildings. Parking lots half-full of compact cars. A church with stained-glass windows. Old people standing on the lawn. Not talking. Just standing and staring off into the general direction of the crotch of an old oak tree, where squirrels and blackbirds were totally plotting things that no one knows about.

On the radio some singer-songwriter guy was whining about broken-down cars and IBM. Dantly punched the radio and turned it off.

"Man, I'm so sick of that fucker. If he hates IBM so much, why's he *singin'* about it? Get over yourself!

Make a goddamn macaroni Christmas ornament or some shit!"

He smoked for a minute. He offered me a lit cigarette and said, "Hey, has Welton talked to you yet?"

"About what?" I asked.

"We're thinking of maybe going down to Iowa City and scorin' a bunch of shrooms. Like several very heavy ounces. Some Dutch poet dude brought them back from Amsterdam. We could sell 'em to the frats at Governors and U.F. Nothing like a little Amsterdamage."

"Where you gonna get the money?"

"Well," he said, "that's where you come in. We were thinking of like robbing the Piggly Wiggly tonight. The one by your crib in E.F. They got like zero surveillance there. A little insta-capital."

The Skylark was so loud, I suddenly realized we had been shouting at each other.

"To do it right, you need three people," he explained. "One to hold 'em up. One to pocket the cash. And one to wait in the car. Like the Father, the Son, and the Holy Ghost. Hang on a second," he said, cutting himself off. He pulled over to the side of the road, shifted into park, opened the door, leaned his head out, and puked. It sounded like he was giving birth through his neck. When he was finished, he turned to me.

"You think you might be interested?"

His nose was suddenly bluer than his teeth.

I was like, "Um. Maybe."

"We were gonna ask this dude Shine from the old folks' home, but he's always falling asleep and shit. Shine and his goddamn K habit. One minute he's scootin' around like a Chihuahua, and the next thing you know he's out cold. Can't have a narcoleptic on the job."

He shifted the Skylark back into gear, and we were moving again.

"I shouldn'ta snorted all that heroin last night," he said, prying something loose from the cracks in his teeth. "I knew it was cut funny. Shit was so yellow, it was almost orange."

He flicked whatever it was that was living between his teeth out the window, and it blew back inside and stuck to the glass over the speedometer. I tried to not stare at it.

"You know who has tolerance?" Dantly asked, clawing at his arm suddenly.

I was like, "Who?"

"Your brother, man. Welton. Welton I-Dealt-One Nugent. That fucker knows when to say when."

I went, "Yeah."

"It's prolly 'cause he used to be this like total jock and shit."

Dantly reached toward the speedometer and fingered the foreign object that had originated between his teeth. For a second I thought he was going to put it back into his mouth in an attempt to start his day over.

"You know," he continued, "I saw your brother play basketball last year, and I didn't even know who he was. It must have been right before he got blindsided with that sciatica shit. East Foote was playing Elizabeth. I was doing some business at the gym—showing this turtleneck sophomore these primo 'ludes I scored when I was living in Portland—and this fucker comes down the court and takes off like a goddamn *air*plane. Like a seven-forty-fuckin'-*seven* or some unnatural thing. I never saw a kid jump so high in my life. I thought you only see animals experience that kind of wind on the Nature Channel. Like spider monkeys or caribou or bionic deer or whatever. Lanky fucker can *jump,* bra."

Dantly took a drag off his cigarette and half of it disappeared.

"And check this," he continued, flicking his ash on his lap. "Last week we're in the parking lot over at Taco John's. I come out with a load of burritos, and the freak is jumping on top of Skyler the Skylark. Jumping on *top* of the motherfucker. The next day, he could hardly walk. I called your house and your dad said he was down in his room icing his back."

"His condition gets pretty bad," I offered.

"The other day at Econofoods, I bump into this very blond cheerleader that Welton used to run around with, and she tells me he was headed to Iowa State before that sciatica shit seized him up. Imagine playing for the *Cyclones* and shit. The Nugents must have some serious bounce runnin' in the family."

I didn't say anything for a minute. I just let the engine buzz through the soles of my Red Wings. I could feel it traveling up the bones in my legs.

"I say we definitely pull off the job in less than three minutes if we exercise the proper aerodynamics," Dantly continued, back on the subject of the robbery. "The butcher, the baker, the candlestick maker—you get what I'm sayin'?"

"Sure," I said.

He was smoking a new cigarette. I hadn't even seen him finish the old one and reload.

"So you in?" he asked.

We were parked in front of Carroll High School now. It was amazing—I had no idea how we'd even gotten there. Dantly's one of those guys who's done so many drugs, he knows about relativity and black holes. I think he knows how to blip in and out of the spaces in the universe.

About eight chicks were pretending to smoke in

175

the parking lot. Two of them were wearing tube tops. One of them looked at Dantly, and he waved. His nose wasn't blue anymore; it was sort of grayish white.

"I'll do it," I said. "But I'm not living at home anymore. I've sort of been crashin' at the old Y."

"Then I'll pick you up there."

I said, "Make it at that little diner next to the civic center. I have sort of a meeting there early in the evening."

"A man with meetings is a mighty man," he sneered. "A mighty, mighty man. How's eight o'clock?"

"Eight's cool," I said, finishing my cigarette.

"You drive, right?" Dantly asked.

"Yeah, I drive."

"Right on. What are you, seventeen, eighteen?"

"Sixteen."

"Six-fuckin'-teen," he sang, shaking his head. "The year of zits and pornos. Here, take one of these," he said, offering a little white tab of paper. It was square and it fit on the tip of my finger. It looked sort of like fish food. Centered on the tab was a small picture of the Cat in the Hat.

"What is it?" I asked.

"It's a little bit of what you can't get today but might want tomorrow."

I looked at it for another second and took it. It dissolved under my tongue and tasted like nothing. Or maybe it tasted sort of metallic. I suddenly felt dull and stupid.

"Beware of the flying fish."

I said, "The flying fish?"

"Yeah, dude. Goldfish mostly. A trout here and there." Then Dantly spit out the window, cleared his throat, and said, "I gotta go score a piece."

I said, "A piece of what?"

"A *piece,* man," he explained. "A fucking gun."

I said, "Oh. Right."

"See you later, bra," Dantly said. "Eight bells."

"Eight bells," I echoed.

That one eye was still closed. Before he took off, I almost reached over and tried to open it.

"Steve Nugent," he said through the window. "Huntin' with the big cats."

When he pulled away, exhaust was everywhere. The whole street was suddenly cloudy with fumes. Joggers fanned the air. Bikers covered their mouths. Birds sprang from trees and flew toward the river.

Halfway down the street, I could still see the smear of vomit blown across the back end of the Skylark.

19

The registration office at Carroll High School smelled like furniture polish and tuna salad.

The elderly lady behind the desk was performing her administrative duties with such thunderstruck slowness it was like she possessed these totally mechanical properties, like she ran on batteries or something.

She finally made eye contact with me after I cleared my throat a few times. I hate doing that, but sometimes you have to. Her makeup had been applied with such severity it was like someone had *forced* her to put it on.

"Can I help you?" she asked. She had one of those kind librarian voices.

I said, "I'd like to register for a summer class."

"Well, you came to the right place. Are you currently enrolled in a local high school?"

I told her that I went to the gifted school and she said, "*Well.* We don't get many of *you* over here in the summer."

"I got this special offer to graduate early if I take a writing class," I explained. "It's sort of like a rebate."

"Oh . . ."

"What's your name?" she asked.

I said, "Steven Nugent."

It's weird how I always tell elderly people that my name is Steven, not Steve. And it *is* Steven; it's just that I never go by that.

"Hello, Steven," she said. "I'm Mrs. Norton. Dee Norton. Pleased to meet you," she said, holding out her hand.

We shook. Her hand sort of trembled and felt pretty fragile.

"You wouldn't happen to be related to *Welton* Nugent, would you?" she asked.

I said, "He's actually my brother."

"Your *brother*," she said. "Well, *that's* exciting. I was at the Carroll–East Foote game last year, and I must say, he's one of the best basketball players I've ever seen. He just *dominated* our boys."

I said, "Yeah, he's pretty good."

"There was even that feature in the paper about him right after the season. The one with the picture of him and your mother."

"Yeah," I said. "He doesn't play anymore."

"Oh," she responded. "Why not?"

I told her about all of his grueling back problems, and she made a face and told me she was sorry to hear that.

Then she started getting together all my paperwork. "I'll just need you to fill out a few forms," she said.

Man, I suddenly wanted a cigarette so bad I thought I was going to die.

"You can come around here and use my desk," she offered.

I came around to the other side of her desk and put my dad's Marine Corps bag under the chair.

On Dee Norton's computer, there was this totally Christian-looking screen saver that read I LIKE ME in cherry-red letters. I watched it blip on and off while she wrestled with the file cabinet.

After she finally got the thing open, she placed about five pieces of paper on her desk in front of me.

"Can I see some ID, Steven?"

I reached into my back pocket, removed my wallet, and gave her my ID from the gifted school. It was all cracked and warped-looking. My mom had saved it from the dryer like nine times. I'd often find it on top of my folded laundry, looking a little more warped each time. In the photo, I still had all my hair and my skin was so white I looked like someone who had frozen to death on the highway.

"Is that *you*?" Mrs. Norton asked.

"Yes, it is."

"Why, you had so much thick, wavy *hair,*" she said, smiling her head off. I was starting to feel sorry for this woman—I really was. I wondered what she was like as a younger woman, if she was pretty and traveled and all of that.

"Now, Steven," she explained, "I have to go down the hall and make a photocopy of your ID. Just fill these out. If you need anything, ask Rosemarie. She's right behind you, in Dr. Derwin's office."

I glanced at all the forms. General Information. Current High School Status. A list of summer courses offered. And some totally random medical form. I filled everything out and sat there tapping my pen on the top of her desk for a minute.

And then, out of nowhere, I sort of grabbed Dee Norton's phone. I dialed nine and the first number that came to mind, which was Mary Mills's number, if you want to know the truth. After four rings, she picked up on the other end.

She said, "Hello?"

Her voice almost knocked the breath out of me.

I said, "Mary?"

And she said, "Yeah?"

"Hey, Mary," I said. "It's, um, Steve."

"Who?"

"Steve," I said. "Steve Nugent."

"White Steve?"

"Yeah," I said. "White Steve. The famous Mathlete."

Her voice suddenly got all small.

"What do you want?" she asked.

"Nothing," I said. "I was just calling to say hi."

Man, when she asked what I wanted, I almost died from the humiliation. I could feel my one cheek blushing like crazy.

In the background, I could hear her TV again. This time it was on a soap opera. Some woman with an exaggerated British accent was begging this totally lethargic-sounding guy to stay with her.

"Steve, you shouldn't be calling me. You really shouldn't."

"Why?" I said.

"Well," she said, "my father sort of thinks you're strange."

"Your father doesn't even know me," I said.

"He knows your brother," she said. "And that guy Dantly."

"Oh," I said.

"So I better go."

"I have to talk to you, Mary," I said with authority. "Like in person."

"Why?"

"I just do. Will you meet me?"

"I can't meet you, Steve."

"Why not?"

"I just can't. Besides, I don't think Shane would be too happy about that."

I said, *"Shane?"*

"Yeah, Shane."

"Shane O'Meara?"

"That's his name, yes."

I said, "Are you like back together with that guy?"

"Well, that's not really any of your business."

"Mary," I said. "You *can't* get back together with him. He's a fucking *mudhead,* man!"

"I'm not a man, Steve."

Suddenly I was smoking. I didn't even realize it. Somehow my hand had started rummaging through my dad's Marine Corps bag and found a pack of Camel Lights and a lighter. My hands lit the cigarette and I was smoking—I really was.

"I gotta go, Steve."

"Meet me tonight, then! I really gotta see you!" I cried, exhaling a great cloud of smoke.

"You scare me, Steve."

"I know. I know I probably totally scare you, but don't be afraid. Don't be afraid at all. I have to tell you something."

"Can't you tell me over the phone?"

"I want to tell you in person."

"Tell me now."

"Okay, I'll tell you now, Mary. I'll totally tell you now. . . ."

I put my cigarette out on Dee Norton's desk—in the potted soil of a dwarf cactus, to be exact—and cleared my throat.

Mary said, "What is it, Steve?"

I took a breath, exhaled, and told her.

I said, "I only have a few weeks to live."

"You do?"

"Yeah," I said. "Ten to fourteen days, actually."

"Why?" she asked. And she was genuinely curious—she really was.

"I have cancer," I said.

"You have cancer?"

"Yes, Mary, I do, I definitely do," I said. "And it feels so good to finally tell someone."

"How long have you known?" she asked.

"It's pretty far advanced," I said. "In the final stages, actually."

"Well, I'm sorry, Steve," she said. "That's very sad."

"I guess I just wanted to tell you," I said.

"Steve," she said, really concerned now, "what kind of cancer is it exactly?"

"Well, brain, actually."

"You have *brain* cancer?"

"Brain cancer, yes." I took a big gulp of air, because when I lie like that, it makes me short of breath. "The center of the tumor—the like *eye* of it or whatever—is multiplying at a pretty alarming rate. I may only have a few more days of consciousness."

"You poor thing. I . . ." she started to say, but she couldn't even finish the sentence because she'd started totally crying right there on the phone. It was one of the most beautiful things I've ever heard.

"Don't cry, Mary," I begged.

"But that's so sad, Steve," she said. "I always thought something might be wrong with you. Because of how pale you are and all. But not *cancer*."

"Don't be sad, Mary. Totally don't be sad."

"I can't help it," she said, and sort of covered the phone so she could blow her nose.

"Will you meet me somewhere?" I tried again.

"Of course," she said. "Of course I'll meet you."

I said, "Cool! Where?"

"I don't know. I sort of have to sneak out. My dad wouldn't be too happy if I told him where I was going."

"How about the Pizza Hut on Kennedy?" I offered.

"Okay," she said. "When?"

"In an hour."

"Okay," she said. "I'll see you there."

Suddenly Dee Norton appeared in the doorway holding my ID and a photocopy. I hung up and drove the butt of my half-smoked Camel Light farther into the soil of her potted cactus.

Dee Norton sniffed the air rabbit-like and went, "Was somebody smoking in here, Steven?"

She stared at me.

I stared back at her.

I could hear her desk clock clipping time.

Finally I said, "There was like this man standing behind me for a moment. I was so steeped in thought, I didn't bother to look. But I could *feel* him, Dee. I believe he *was* smoking."

Man, once you start lying, you just can't stop. It's totally addictive.

"Oh, that Dr. Derwin," she said, shaking her head. "He's always trying to sneak one when I scoot out. Our own principal bending the rules. That habit belongs in the teachers' lounge."

"I couldn't agree more," I said. "And you look great, by the way," I offered.

"Why, thank you, Steven," she said, picking a piece of lint off of her blouse. "I'm sorry it took me so long with your ID. The copier kept getting jammed."

She took my paperwork off the desk and started arranging it in a file folder.

"So you said you needed a writing class?" Dee Norton asked.

"Yeah, creative writing."

"Well, Mr. Stevens has a class that meets once a week on Wednesday mornings from nine till eleven. That's the only one we offer."

"That's perfect," I said.

"Okay, then. I'll just need to talk to your parents to sort out the billing. Should I call your mother?"

"I don't think that would be a very good idea."

"Why not?"

"Um. Because she's like in the middle of this very important quilting tournament. She shouldn't be disturbed. But call my dad. He's probably at home right now."

"What's his name?"

"His name is Richard," I said. "Richard Nugent. You can call him Dick."

"Dick?"

"Yeah, totally call him Dick. He's probably like watching a fucking game show or something."

"Excuse me, but there's no need for that kind of language, Steven."

"I'm sorry, Dee," I said. And I was—I really was. I had no idea what was flying out of my mouth, and it was just getting worse and worse. "You're so right. It's the medication, you know? I'm totally sorry, man—I mean *ma'am*. Sorry, *ma'am*."

"What medication?"

It was getting so bad, I was forgetting what lie I was telling to who.

"Just this stuff I have to take."

She looked at me suspiciously and started marking up my forms with a ballpoint pen.

"Your father doesn't have e-mail, does he?" she asked.

"No," I said. "Dick doesn't even have snail mail."

"I'll call him, then."

She looked at me for a long moment and said, "Are you okay? You're looking a little sleepy."

Dr. Seuss was finally kicking in. I felt like I was wearing fluffy pajamas. Those ones with the little vinyl feet.

Dee Norton felt my forehead. Her hand was tiny

and wet. Her wrist smelled like flowers and talcum powder.

"I better go," I said, standing up. The world was suddenly a funhouse.

"Okay. Well, I'll see you around school, then."

"See you around," I said.

"And give your brother my best. I'll pray for his recovery."

I grabbed my dad's Marine Corps bag and left.

In the hallway, this old janitor was mopping the floor.

I stood there and watched him for a minute. He rinsed the mop with such care, I thought he would start singing to it or something.

"Hey," I shouted to him. The word just flew out of my mouth.

He looked up.

I said, "Knock, knock."

He said, "What?"

I said, "*Knock, knock,* man!"

"Oh," he answered. "Who's there?"

He had a voice like an old rusty hacksaw.

"I-got."

"I-got who?" he asked, playing along nicely.

"I got cancer, what about you?"

He didn't say anything. He just stood there and looked at me.

"Brain cancer," I added, but he just kept staring at me.

For some reason, I wanted more from him, so I pretended I had a gun in my dad's Marine Corps bag. What I did was I put my hand in the bag and pointed my finger and lifted the bag up like I was aiming it at him.

"Put your hands up," I commanded, and he did; he really did. He put them up and the mop dropped to the floor. We stayed like that for like a minute, and then I lowered the bag to my side and pulled my hand out.

Then for some reason I said, "My mom had this dream that my brother was at the circus and his pants kept falling down."

He still didn't know what to say, so he just stared at me. I was starting to feel even weirder, almost invincible, like I could take on anything, so I left.

20

So in group today, Dr. Shays talked about the difference between humans and animals and what he called the "divine order of things," which, in his words, starting from the bottom of that weird food chain, goes rocks, plants, animals, humans, angels, and God. He then talked about the differences between each—the like distinctions or whatever—and how making choices is the thing that separates the human from all of those forms below it. He seemed to get sort of passionate about the subject, like maybe he's spent too much time with his rock collection or something. When he asked us to share, I raised my hand for the first time since I came to Burnstone Grove.

"Steven," he said. "What's on your mind?"

"About this whole divine order of things. I have this theory," I said.

I looked over at Silent Starla, and she sort of half grinned at me with knowing eyes.

"A theory," he said, sort of smiling. He wasn't being condescending; he really wasn't. "Please share," he continued.

So what I launched into was this realization I'd had on the way to meeting Mary Mills. It was no doubt inspired by the tab of acid that Dantly had given me. And this was what I tried to articulate to the best of my ability: "We were all plants once," I said. "Not apes or birds or sea creatures. Plants. Our arms and legs were leaves. Our spines stems. God urinated on all the dominions of vegetation and the plants turned into people."

While confirming these evolutionary and spiritual certainties, I spoke to the group slower than I ever have spoken in my life.

"We ran right out of the earth and never looked back," I continued on. "Animals were moss," I explained. "And fish were sort of these mushroomy things. So to be human is to be rootless," I said. "We're not meant to be held down by mortgage payments or microwave dinners or pets. We're basically meant to totally like *ambulate* and eat a lot of hamburgers."

Everyone stared at me sort of in awe. It was pretty cool, I must admit.

"And when did you come up with all of this?" Dr. Shays asked, more amused than stirred.

"Last summer," I said. "After I dropped acid for the first time."

This got a pretty big laugh from the rest of the members of the group. Silent Starla was particularly amused, and she sort of licked her lips and smiled at me.

But it was true. I did come up with all of that on my way to meeting Mary Mills. My thoughts were like giant hot-air balloons full of truths I'd never known.

As I crossed to the other side of Kennedy, the Pizza Hut's illuminated sign seemed to expand. I had this beautiful feeling that everyone inside knew I was coming.

Welcome, Steve!

Won't you join us for a snack and a beverage?

We have a beautiful salad bar full of crispy croutons!

When I entered the Pizza Hut, about four families stopped eating and just stared at me.

I felt like I suddenly had two million teeth and I couldn't stop grinning.

This very managerial-looking guy was wiping down the salad bar. He was working so hard it was like someone was manipulating him with remote control. When he glanced up, this totally 3-D goldfish squirted out of his mouth and took flight over the multiplying families. It was Dantly's goldfish. I closed my eyes and opened them again. There was a lion lounging on the salad bar and it was wearing plaid golf pants!

I said, *"Whoa . . ."*

The manager guy moved toward me the way one moves toward a person who has caught on fire and doesn't know it. It must have been my record-setting grin. Or maybe it was the way I was using the Ms. Pac-Man game to keep myself from falling.

The families were multiplying at an alarming rate.

The manager said, "Can I hold you?"

I said, *"What?"*

He hiked his belt up and said, "I said, 'Can I help you?'" He was nice about it—he really was.

Someone was totally screwing with his voice. Through the soles of my Red Wings I could totally feel my feet reaching for the earth underneath the concrete underneath the Pizza Hut.

I went, "Um. Yeah. I'm gonna like meet someone. A girl. Real pretty girl."

"Well, son, in your state I'm afraid I'm going to have to ask you to wait outside."

"Steve?" a voice rang out.

The manager whirled.

I whirled.

Children turned into panda bears.

Their mothers into washing machines.

The entire restaurant spun like a salad bowl.

It was the lion from the salad bar. It was a lioness

now. The lioness dismounted and turned into Mary Mills from the gifted school.

The floating goldfish evaporated.

The pandas entered the washing machines.

"He's with me," Mary Mills told the manager, taking my dad's Marine Corps bag, which I had left on the Ms. Pac-Man machine, and then my frozen arm. She led me to her booth and I sat.

Mary Mills sat across from me.

Her hair was black.

Her eyes were green.

Her skin was really white.

She was a painting. Like something stolen from one of those museums in Europe. A talking painting. I was really impressed.

Mary said, "I only have forty minutes."

She could have said, "I just opened a savings account," or "I happened to step in a dog turd on Thursday." It didn't matter. The fact is she *spoke*. To *me*.

We slid on the vinyl upholstery.

Our movements were slow and ballet-like.

I could feel my mouth hanging open. I was like a dog under the supper table.

I suddenly realized that I had popped this totally vertical erection that would rival any I'd ever had. My hands trembled slightly. I could hear myself panting.

Under the table I adjusted my erection with my left hand. It was firm and angular.

"I ordered you a personal pan pizza with sausage," Mary Mills offered. "I hope that's okay."

"It's perfect," I said.

She sort of shifted a bit and said, "What's in the bag?"

"Um," I said, "just a few important possessions."

"Are you warm?"

"I'm warm."

"Are you comfortable?"

"I'm comfortable."

"Is there anything I can do?"

She took my hand. It was trembling so much, I was afraid it would start like *shrinking* or something.

"Do your mom and dad even know you're here?" Mary asked, still clutching my hand.

"No," I said. "I sort of sneaked away."

"Your poor parents," Mary Mills said, setting her glass down, breathing, breathing. "How have they been handling it?"

I was like, "Everyone's been pretty cool. They all realize it's pretty late in the game."

Then there was a lull in the conversation. But she was still holding my hand; she really was. My hallucinations had subsided for a minute and I was suddenly acutely aware of how incredibly unreal everything felt.

I said, "Hey, would you go see a movie with me later?"

"Steve," she said suddenly, setting her glass down, not bothering to answer. "I want you to know something. And this is sort of hard for me to say."

"Okay," I said.

"Well," she said. Her eyes were really huge and beautiful. "I just wanted to tell you that I forgive you."

"Forgive me?" I said. "Forgive me for what exactly?"

"For that day at school last year. For what you did. To me."

I said, "Um, what I did to you when?"

"Outside the music room. When I was at the water fountain."

"What did I do?"

"Well, you touched me, Steve. Very inappropriately, I might add. You stroked my . . . well, my butt, actually."

I said. "I'm sorry, Mary. I'm really really sorry."

Mary Mills drank again and set her glass down.

She was like, "Sometimes, I think about that day, and . . ."

"And what?"

"Well, I used to wonder if . . ."

"If *what,* Mary?" I pleaded. "If *what?*"

"Well, if things might have worked out differently."

I was like, "Differently?"

"Yes. If we could have become better friends if you didn't, well, *touch* me like that. I mean, I actually thought you had potential. Steve, you have so much anger inside you."

"I do?"

"Steve," she went on, "this next question might seem a little weird to you, but I have to ask it."

"What, Mary?" I said. "What?"

"Do you believe in God?"

I said, "Like *God* God?"

"Yes," she said. "God God."

I was like, "Um. God is like *dog* spelled backward."

Suddenly the waiter was standing over us like a funeral director. He was two thousand years old, and he had this totally Dungeons & Dragons–looking horse's tail. He placed my personal pan pizza down in front of me, as well as a pitcher of Coke.

Mary and I were silent now. The talk of God was over.

I ate my personal pan pizza in about two minutes flat. I didn't even realize how hungry I was.

In between mouthfuls, I was like, "Mary, you ever play Marco Polo?"

"What's that?" she asked.

"That game you play in a swimming pool. It's kind of like tag. Whoever's 'it' has to keep his eyes closed. He sort of treads water and says 'Marco' and everyone else says 'Polo,' and using his other senses, he has to figure out where they are in the pool."

Mary said, "I have no idea what you're talking about."

"Sure you do, Mary. Sure you do."

"I've never played it."

I went, "It's like tag, man! Like tag!"

"*Okay.*" she said. "Jesus, Steve."

"Let's play right now," I managed to say in between mouthfuls. "Just me and you."

"We can't, Steve."

"But we can, Mary. We totally *can.*"

"We're not even in a *pool.*"

"Use your imagination, Mary. Give that noodle of yours something to grapple with."

"You're starting to frighten me, Steve."

I was like, "What about Red Rover? That's a great game! All those kids locking their arms. The summoned preteen getting slammed in the neck by an angry knot of bony arms. Let's play, Mary. Me against you. One-on-one. Red Rover, Red Rover, send *Mary* right over."

"Steve, I understand you're under a lot of stress with your condition and all, but I'm afraid I just can't start playing games with you. And certainly not violent ones. Under the circumstances, I think it would be silly!"

"You know, Mary, if you like say 'violence' with a lazy Louisiana accent it sounds like 'violins'?"

"I'm starting to feel very uncomfortable. I should have known this couldn't be normal."

"You know, you're right, Mary. You're totally right and I'm sorry. You're a thousand percent correct, so I have a better idea."

"What?"

"Let's just cut the game idea and admit that we're each others' density."

"*Density?*"

"I mean *des*tiny."

"Steve, I want you to take this," she said, handing me something wrapped in tissue. It was small and fit in my hand. I stopped eating and started to unwrap it.

"Wipe your hands, please."

I wiped my hands with my napkin and tore off the tissue paper. It was a small ceramic figurine of a man wearing a blue robe. He had a very well-groomed beard and amazing hair. His palm was thrust out as if he was blessing someone.

"What is it?" I asked.

"It's a statuette of Saint Bonaventure."

I said, "Oh. Who's that?"

"He's famous for ridding a town of a bothersome wolf. He was Scottish, I think. He's a kind of protector. My mother brought it home the day after our house got broken into."

"When did that happen?"

"About a week ago. The burglar came in through the downstairs patio doors while we were sleeping. My dad forgot to lock them before he went to bed."

"What did he do?"

"Well, not much, actually. He ate a bowl of cereal and stole my mother's Pennsylvania Dutch spirit plate."

I said, "Whoa."

"And I think he was wounded, because there was blood tracked all over the linoleum in the kitchen. I woke up the next morning and cleaned it all up. I thought it was from my dad. He's always doing things in the garage with power tools and stuff."

Mary Mills stopped a moment and drank her water.

"It was weird," she added. "The burglar could have cleaned us out, but he didn't."

My erection had gone away and I could feel the need to urinate totally threading through my bladder.

"It's odd," Mary continued, "you almost got the feeling that the burglar wanted to *stay the night* or something. Like he was lonely. I mean, that whole cereal thing is so childlike. The police say that if I would have left the blood, they could have had better evidence. DNA and that kind of stuff."

I was like, "Man, thanks, Mary."

"Thanks?"

"Totally."

"Thanks for what, Steve?"

"Oh. For the *statue*!" I declared, thrusting Saint Bonaventure in the air with a power fist.

"My mom was keeping him above the fridge, but I don't understand the point. I mean, my dad just installed a five-thousand-dollar infrared alarm system that's linked to the police precinct. Somehow it seems more appropriate for you to have him. He'll watch over you, Steve."

"So they never caught the guy?" I asked.

"No. There wasn't enough evidence. Only a few smudged fingerprints."

I started laughing for some reason. I cackled like a ghoul. I laughed so hard it felt like my teeth would fall out.

I looked up and realized that everyone was watching us.

"What's so funny?" Mary Mills asked.

I was like, "What?"

"Why are you laughing?"

I went, "I'm not laughing."

I was laughing so hard I thought my stomach was going to burst.

Mary's face fell.

She said, "And the quality of your laughter is so . . . *weird*."

I went, "What—you think I'm like on *acid* or something?"

"No."

"You think I like dropped a few hits before I met you?"

"Of course not, Steve."

I completely lost it after that.

Our waiter was conspiring with the woman behind the cash register, who was conspiring with the manager. I was laughing so hard it was totally tickling my bladder.

The manager was on his way over now.

"Steve, why are you *laughing*?" Mary asked, sounding genuinely scared now.

I said, "'Cause I'm like pissing my pants."

She went, "You are?"

"Uh-huh. Ah-huh-huh-*huh-huh-huh*. . . ."

And it was true: I *was* totally urinating in my pants. It was amazing. If you ever want to change your life immediately, just sit down in some random fast-food place and start urinating in your pants. My lap was all wet and warm, and it was running down my legs and filling my Red Wing boots.

I even told the manager. I said, "I'm totally pissing my pants, man. Sorry."

The manager twiddled the ends of his mustache.

He went, "Well, that's just not very sanitary, son." Now I was his son. "I'm afraid I'm going to have to ask you to leave."

"Whatever, Dad," I said. I was his son, so he was obviously my dad, right?

We were one big happy Pizza Hut family.

I turned back to Mary and said, "And the thing about it, Mary? The thing about it is that I could like stop pissing right now, but I don't want to 'cause it's so like *warm*."

"He's sick," Mary explained to the manager.

"Yeah," I said. "I'm sick. Sick as a dog. *Marco!*" I called out to all the families. They were all stuffing their faces. "Come on everyone!" I shouted. *"Marco!"*

"I have to go, Steve," Mary said. "I'm sorry."

"Son, I'm afraid you're going to have to leave," the manager said. "I'm prepared to call the authorities."

"No problem, Dad!"

"I'm sorry, Steve," Mary said, sliding out of our booth and leaving a twenty on the table. "Keep the change."

She stood. I attempted to stand but my legs were suddenly two thousand pounds each.

"Marco!" I shouted again, but no one would return my call. They were all being shy.

"I'm sorry we were so disruptive, sir," Mary told the manager, but he just stood there with his arms folded at his chest.

"Good luck, Steve," Mary Mills said. I reached out for her, but she turned and left.

I sat there for a moment and smelled the urine rising out of my lap. Everyone was still staring at me.

"Let's go, son," the manager said again.

I grabbed my dad's Marine Corps bag and held it for a moment. Somehow it felt like I was holding my own head. I would unzip the bag and there I would be, grinning right back at me.

Man, I don't even remember leaving the Pizza Hut. All I know is that my crotch was soaked and my head felt like a helium balloon that was trying to float off into the sky.

The traffic on Kennedy was strange and noiseless. I could see birds perched on streetlights. Big black crows. I had this weird feeling that they wanted me, these birds. They would swoop down and start pecking away at my skull.

While Mary Mills was walking out of the Pizza Hut, I think she had tears in her eyes. Nothing dramatic. The kind you can barely see.

21

I had forgotten how good a Camel Light could taste. I smoked half a pack on my way back downtown.

When I reached Foote University, I sat down on the sidewalk and pulled a rock out of my Red Wings. It took about five minutes to undo my laces. My hands were so slow, it was like I had frostbite or something.

Moments later a bell tower tolled deliriously. My mom always called the ones from St. Rose of Lima's the evening vespers. "Listen to the evening vespers," she'd say from her hospice bed. "You can hear them all the way over in Foote."

I turned and stared out over Foote University. It was empty as a cemetery. It somehow looked like you would get shot if you tried to run across campus.

I finally got my boot on and headed back down Governors Boulevard.

Through the window of a barbershop, I could see these three elderly men getting shaves. They were all leaning their heads back and it looked all weird and sexual.

I couldn't light a new cigarette fast enough.

Dr. Seuss was hitting me in waves. One minute a tree was simply a tree, and then I would blink and it would change into an ostrich wearing a football helmet. And then into an enormous bear paw. The acid was doing strange things to my Camel Lights, too. I would exhale clouds of green paint. Then it was gold. And then it was black. I could blend if I smoked two at a time. Red and blue makes purple.

I could suddenly hear birds.

I could hear the buzzing of power lines.

I could hear insects in a bush.

The low Foote skyline looked like some little kid had cut it out of construction paper.

The downtown area was totally dead-looking. Everything was closed and there wasn't a soul on the street. It had the eerie feeling of a place where a bomb had vaporized all living creatures, only to spare the buildings and parking meters.

The first thing I did when I got to Jack Palomino's was hit the bathroom. I changed out of my underwear and threw the wet ones in the trash. I had forgotten to pack an extra pair of jeans, so I peeled off the ones I was wearing, rinsed the urine out of them in the sink, and attempted to dry them under the hand blower.

While I was drying my pants, I stared at the backs of my hands. My arms. My chest. I didn't even realize it, but I was totally naked! Somewhere between rinsing my jeans and holding them in front of the hand blower, I had managed to remove *all* my clothes! Even my socks were off!

My arms were long and veiny. My chest was so skinny you could have stuck a safety pin clear through me. My nipples were the same color as my skin. My bellybutton was a piece of dirty popcorn. There were flecks of blue paint all over my neck. I basically looked like some freak in a horror movie.

After a few dry cycles, for some reason I started sort of staring at my crotch in the mirror. Man, I was sixteen and bald as a Frisbee. I was six three, but I had the genitals of a prepubescent snowman. The final stages of puberty were avoiding me the way girls in cars avoid looking at you on the highway.

What happened was I started getting pretty angry. All those guys in the locker room with their hairy underarms! Throwing bars of soap to each other! Spraying aerosol deodorant into their totally bearded pits! Brad McGwire and his shaving habit, always smelling like his dad's Old Spice! Todd Lindholm, the spelling champ with his chiseled, perfectly carpeted chest! That five-foot-four-inch freshman tuba player with the pubic mound so thick and curly it made my scrotum shrivel just thinking about it!

I was tired of being that one guy in the shower room after gym class—the towel-line fugitive who makes a beeline right for his locker! I was through with waiting for my hormones to thaw out of their freeze-dried paralysis!

So I figured it was finally time.

I let my jeans fall to the floor. I took the black permanent marker out of my dad's Marine Corps bag and drew on a bush. I used slow, careful strokes. My hands were shaking again, but I figured it would make for good frizz effect.

I realized I was in the women's bathroom when this totally thunderstruck-looking, heavyset waitress came blasting through the toilet stall. She screamed so loud I thought the mirror would shatter. The bathroom suddenly spun like a casino game. I rifled through my dad's Marine Corps bag, and in a very elastic, multifaceted move, slid into a pair of Robitussin-drenched underwear. I stepped into my damp jeans and Red Wings with the grace of a wounded giraffe. When I started for the door, I slipped and landed on my knees and the pain shot up my femurs. I got to my feet and stumbled out of the bathroom.

The diner was hot and smelled like bleach and bacon.

"Steve!" a voice sang out.

It was June. She was wearing the same shirt from the day before—that one with the pickle on it. She was kneeling in a booth.

"June," I called to her feebly.

"You look *terrible,*" she said.

"I had sort of a rough night," I explained.

"Let's eat and then we'll discuss our future," she announced.

"He ain't eatin' in here," the heavyset waitress ruled, suddenly appearing from behind the counter. Man, she was pissed about what had happened in the bathroom.

"Sorry about that," I offered, but the waitress just sort of stared at me like I was highly contagious or something.

"Let's go to Mickey D's," June said, pinching my arm and then twisting. "I'll buy you a combo."

22

On the street, June whirled.

"Check out my new move," she said, snap-kicking the air in front of her. An invisible foe fell to the pavement. June pumped her fist victoriously. She repeated the move and continued walking.

I was like, "Wow. Where'd you learn that?"

"Five Deadly Venoms."

"Five Deadly Venoms?"

"It's a kung-fu movie. I'm still working on my centipede. Eljay can do the monkey-style without popping back up."

"Who's Eljay?"

"My mom's boyfriend. He's cool. He bought me a PlayStation II for Easter. Sometimes he lets me use his cell phone. He owns a speedboat."

We headed toward McDonald's at a slow pace. The sun was starting to lapse into the horizon. It was sort of this bloody orange color and looked flattened, like it had been kicked. The humidity was starting to feel like something that was always there now. It hadn't let up all day.

My feet ached and my jeans were really irritating. I walked like there were thumbtacks in my boots.

I'm convinced that the acid was tweaking out my emotions. Every time I took a breath, I thought I'd start crying.

"Is your mom picking you up later?" I asked June.

"Yeah," she said, skipping ahead a few paces, "but we got time. Her and Eljay went to Cedar Rapids today."

"What's in Cedar Rapids?" I asked.

"Who knows? Maybe a new dancin' gig."

We walked. The sky was filled with sickly gray clouds. June did another snap-kick, almost taking out a parking meter. She backed up suddenly, playfully throwing a hip into my leg. "I told her about you," she said. Her voice got a little flirty when she said that.

I was like, "You did?"

"Yop. It's funny 'cause she thinks you're like twelve or somethin'."

I was like, "Um, like what did you tell her exactly?"

"Nothin'," she said, skipping ahead again. June had about five gears going.

"Hey!" she offered, turning back around. "A ham sandwich walks into a bar and orders a drink. What does the bartender say?"

"I don't know," I said. "What?"

"Sorry, buddy. We don't *serve* ham sandwiches here! Get it?"

I was like, "Totally got it."

"Can I bum a square?" June asked.

I reached into my dad's Marine Corps bag and fished out a Camel Light. June snatched it out of my hand and rolled it between her fingers. I lit it and she smoked.

When we reached McDonald's, we sat down outside at the same picnic table we'd used the previous day.

"I'll be right back," June said, taking a long drag on her cigarette, then flicking the butt several yards. "Whuddaya want?" she asked.

"Um. Maybe just an apple pie."

"That's it?"

"I guess."

"You don't want no fries?"

"Not really."

"But you need vitamins. Nutriments and stuff. Fries got vitamins, Steve."

"You can have all my vitamins."

"Suit yourself," she said, turning and half skipping into the McDonald's.

I looked in through the brown window. There were about eight families stuffing their faces with burgers and fries and Chicken McNuggets. They were all wearing bright T-shirts and cargo shorts. The T-shirts were blue or red or yellow and they all had pockets. It was sort of like they had all called each other at home to arrange a wardrobe theme for a post-McDonald's fun-photo.

June sort of spun through the tables on her way toward the front and did a cartwheel just before she got to the ordering counter, almost clocking this dad in the head.

A blade of pain rotated in my stomach. I hadn't even been away from home for two days, and I felt like I had aged like twenty years or something.

From my dad's Marine Corps bag, I removed Saint Bonaventure. Somehow I knew he would have answers. He was a saint, after all. I stared at him for a long time. He looked sort of bored and tired. *Saints have to work harder than this,* I thought. *They can't give up just because some wolf is giving them a hard time.*

"Saint Bonaventure," I said, "what's it all about, anyway?"

I waited for him to answer but he didn't respond, so I shook him a little.

I shouted, "Come on, Bonnie!"

He still wouldn't respond, so I thwacked him in the head a few times.

When he spoke, for some reason he possessed a slight Australian accent, I swear.

"What's *what* all about, mate?" he answered back.

I was like, "I don't know, Bonnie. *All* of it."

"All of what, mate?"

"The *reason,* man. Like the moon and stuff. Like water and fish and twenty-foot speedboats and the Internet and—and—and—and like *girls*!" I practically screamed. "I mean, what's the whole point of it all, Bonnie?"

"The point?"

"Yeah, man," I said, "the *point.*"

He chuckled a bit and went, "You tell me, mate."

"I mean, you get like totally pooped out into the world, and all you do is eat cheeseburgers and watch shampoo commercials and wait for Christmas and take tests and learn derivatives and what's x and what's y and then there's limits and sine and cosine and SATs and e-mail and those cell phones that display your stock options and all the college brochures with those sad girls in those totally varsity-looking sweaters—"

"Um. Who are you talking to?"

I looked up. It was June. She was holding an apple pie out in front of her. It might as well have been a brick, the way she was holding it. I glanced down at Saint Bonaventure and waited for him to say something else, but he'd already turned back into a statuette.

I took the apple pie from June, and she sat down on the other side of the picnic table and started feasting on a supersize two-cheeseburger combo and an orange pop.

For some reason, I started feeling really paranoid. Maybe it was the way June was eating. She was suddenly so interested in her food, it made me feel totally insecure. To tell you the truth, it sort of made me feel like I was disappearing.

For some reason I was like, "June, can I ask you a question?"

She went, "You just did, but ask me another one."

I took a breath. "Do you think I'm crazy?"

June swallowed another fry and went, "*Eljay's* the crazy one. He carries this monkey wrench in the back of his Beemer. I seen him beat a tree with it once. There was a birdhouse in it, too. He beat the tree so bad, the birdhouse fell and broke on the sidewalk. *That's* crazy, Steve. You're just lonely."

June just stared off, drinking her pop. The sun was almost gone, and the sky over the river looked dirty.

"You're a very confused and disturbed individual, Steve."

"I know, June," I said. "I'm usually not so disturbed, but right now I totally am."

217

"Maybe you should like see a shrink or somethin'."

"No way. Shrinks are total con artists," I said. Which is what I truly believed at the time. I'm sure Dr. Shays or Mrs. Leene won't feel too thrilled about that statement, but it's really how I felt back then. Mrs. Leene, if you're reading this, you're an exception to the rule.

"My mom sees one," June continued. "She goes to Alcoholics Anonymous, too. That's where she met Eljay."

I pictured her mom and Eljay slow dancing at some AA singles' meetings, her mom in some cheap dress from the mall and Eljay in a sharkskin suit, his big monkey wrench propped on his shoulder. I know that's not fair of me imagining them that way, but when I closed my eyes, that's what I saw, I swear.

Then June said, "Let's talk about something else, okay?"

"Okay," I said, but I didn't know what to talk about. For some reason I started thinking about Mary Mills again. How we almost had a moment at the Pizza Hut. How she really did feel sorry for me.

I said, "What *is* it about girls, June?"

"Oh, brother," she said, finishing my apple pie.

"I mean, these days you have to be this total country-western singer to score. Either that or some kind of offensive lineman with a Jeep and the windows have to be like totally *smoked* or whatever. I mean, come on, I know I'm not Hercules or Garth Brooks or—or—*or*—or—*or* Sammy fucking *So*sa. Hell, I'm not even that guy on the news—the one with the totally blow-dried hair."

"Storm Field?"

"Yeah, Storm Field. The weatherman with the hair. I'm not even *that.* But I'm pretty cool. I mean I'm tall, right?"

"Tall's a handsome feature."

"I got a good set of teeth. I have cool clothes."

"Yeah," she said, "I like how you never change 'em."

She was totally dead-on with that observation, especially then, but I didn't let it derail me.

"And when I *had* hair," I continued, "it was well tended to and I didn't have dandruff or anything."

June said, "I had lice once. My mom made me take this bath in medicine. It smelled like Reynolds Wrap and chicken."

I plowed on.

"I guess it's all about Jeeps and stomach muscles and the thickness of your neck."

June smiled and said, "*I'm* a girl."

"Yeah, but you're like four, June."

"I'm gonna be *eleven,* Steve. *Eleven.*"

"Yeah, but—"

"Eleven's not four!"

"What is it with you beasts?"

"I'm not a beast!" June cried. Then she pinched me.

"Ouch!" I cried. It really did sort of hurt, but I continued on.

I said, "I mean, take kissing for instance. You can practice for months. Like on an apple or a pear or a *toaster oven* or whatever. You can practice till your lips practically *fall off,* and it doesn't make one bit of difference. The minute—no, the second, the absolute *second* you get the opportunity, all of that practice—all of those apples and pears and toaster ovens fly right out the window."

"Are you gonna try to kiss me, Steve?"

"No, June," I said. "No way. I'm not gonna try to kiss you."

That's when something really weird happened. I'm not sure if it was all that Robitussin in my crotch or another wave of Dr. Seuss taking effect, but I looked at June and she started turning into Mary Mills. The black hair. The green eyes. The perfect skin.

"Red Rover, Red Rover, send *MARY* right over!" I blurted.

June-slash-Mary said, "What?"

"Come on, Mary, play along!" I cried.

Then I was going after her, like I was totally trying to *capture* her or something. And she was countering my every move. We were sort of enacting this slightly playful but also slightly desperate game of catch-me-if-you-can around the picnic table. It was our most romantic moment yet. I felt myself swipe at her. In fact, just as I grazed her hair, Mary-slash-June turned into my mom. Her teeth went sort of blue and her hair fell out and her eyes dulled to the color of pork grease. Her lips got all small and dry, too.

"Go to St. Rose's, Steven, honey. Go to St. Rose's and light a candle for me," I heard her say.

We stared at each other for a moment, and then just as she reached for me, I was out of there. I turned and ran, my free arm pumping, my dad's Marine Corps bag sort of rattling behind me.

"Steve," I heard. "Wait! What about the movies?!"

I ran down an alley. It had a dead end, so I turned around and chose a different alley. I ran through garbage heaps and stacks of newspapers and something that looked like a person. I jumped over a collection of pop bottles. I heard a dog barking and knew for sure it was in pursuit of me. Then I stopped and leaned up against a very mossy-feeling wall and vomited like nothing I had ever experienced before. I won't describe it, don't worry. When I was finished, I pushed away from the wall and started walking again. My feet felt like they weighed two hundred pounds each. I vomited again while I was walking. Then I tripped over a box of recycling hopefuls and vomited while I was tripping. Then I stood and then I went to a knee and then I stood again and then I went back down to a knee and vomited a final time in a strange sort of genuflection.

Somehow I wound up back at the diner. It was almost dark now, and all the streetlights were on. Dantly's Skylark was parked in front, the engine idling. The headlights were off and I could see Dantly's and my brother's heads framed in the windshield.

The engine was running, but as I drew closer, I could see that they were actually sleeping. Dantly's head was lolled back on the headrest, and he was sort of snoring. Welton was seated in the passenger's side and he had this totally gleeful smile on his face.

I looked back at Dantly, and I could see a handgun peeking out of the front of his jeans.

The Skylark belched, and the motor started running faster. Dantly's foot must have accidentally pressed on the gas. Welton shifted his position on the passenger's side. That's when I pushed away from the car. The steel door radiated into my palms for a moment and then, just like that, I was facing the other direction and sort of jogging away. My shin was killing me and I was starting to limp.

I jog-limped around the corner and ducked into another alley. There was a fire escape full of potted plants and broken toys and bicycle parts and stacks of spoiled newspapers.

I sat under the fire escape and stared up at the darkening sky. It was that weird, flattened hour when God or whoever it is up there decides your fate. It's not quite night but the day is definitely over. This is when he either ruins your life or snaps his fingers and—*POW!*—things suddenly change for the better.

In the distance I heard a car horn. It honked three times, sort of desperately, and the final honk went on a little too long. It was my last chance to come out of the alley, but I couldn't move.

I pulled my dad's Marine Corps bag close and just let my head fall back against the alley wall. After a minute I could hear the car pulling away.

23

So Shannon Lynch has to leave because he got caught trying to kiss this new Blue Grouper from Griffith, Indiana, named Jason Gilecki.

It pains me to know this information for a myriad of reasons, and I will name three. First, he was my best friend here at Burnstone Grove. Second, I feel like maybe he was just using our friendship so he could see if he could kiss me. Third, if he's gay, he should just say that he's gay and not worry what people think, because he's incredibly cool and it wouldn't matter. Silent Starla told me about it after we made out in the common room. We were alone and she had been chewing grape gum.

"He totally tried to put his mouth on Jason's," she said.

"Did Jason kiss him back?" I asked.

"Well, obviously *not,* seeing as he narked on him."

"So where are they sending him?" I asked.

"To this place in Lake Geneva, Illinois, called Unity House. It's mostly junkies at that one."

"He tried to kiss me, too," I told Silent Starla.

"I figured," she said. "He's such a ho. He does that trick where he puts all that change up his nose and he sort of lures you in. And then he starts talking about Sam Shepard and Harold Pinter and the theater and he gets all the straight boys to go all gaga over how cool he is and then before you know it, he's laid one on you. Am I right?"

I didn't answer because it was totally true.

"That's okay," she said. "You don't have to answer that. Did you kiss him back?"

"Sort of," I said.

"So are you like bi or something?"

"No," I said. "He sort of took me by surprise."

"And you're still friends?"

"Yes," I said.

"That's big of you," she said, and then we started kissing again. It was weird, though, because even though Shannon kissing me did take me by surprise and it did sort of suck, I think it made me a better kisser somehow, I really do, so I have to give the guy a little credit, right?

After about two minutes, Silent Starla stopped again.

"Do you want to have sex with me?" she asked.

I said, "Really?" and then I swallowed like six times.

"Yeah, really," Silent Starla said.

225

"Wow," I said.

"If you don't want to, just say it."

"No, I do," I said. "I totally do."

"So let's go," she said, and then she took my hand and led me to this weird maintenance room on the other side of the cafeteria. Man, was I nervous. I don't think I'd ever been that nervous in my whole life.

The room was mostly cement and it smelled like that pink liquid soap they use in all the Burnstone Grove bathrooms.

"No one will find us here," Silent Starla said.

"What about the maintenance workers?"

"They got off like twenty minutes ago."

Then she turned the light off and removed her shirt. Her breasts were maybe the best things I've ever felt in my life. Sort of soft and round, and her nipples were highly aroused. Someone had forgotten to turn off this clip light on the other side of the room. It was on pretty dim, but I could still see her pretty good.

"Call me Sinead," she said while she ran her hands through my hair, which has grown out enough by now to actually grab onto a bit, which she was doing, which was making everything even more masterful than it already was.

"Sinead," I said, kissing her breasts, "Sinead."

Then she took my clothes off—all of them—just

226

like that, and I was standing there naked, trying to sort of cover my erection, when she started touching me. At first she sort of touched my stomach and then she touched my knees and then she touched the scar on my shin and then she did some other stuff that I won't gross you out with, and then she took her clothes off, and she has a pretty masterful body, I must say, and her pubic hair was nice and trim and sort of glistening, and then she produced a condom from some unknown region and then she was putting it on me and then she leaned back and sort of pulled me on top of her and she made me touch her between her legs for a while and then she pushed my hand away and put my penis inside of her and we made love.

I only lasted like four minutes, and I really had no idea what I was doing, but Sinead guided me through it and she was incredibly helpful. And even though I was probably about as suave as a blind three-legged mule, we still *did it* and I officially lost my virginity and now I am in love with a girl named Sinead who everyone knows as Silent Starla.

While stretched out on the cold cement floor, I asked her why she tried to kill herself.

"I don't know," she said. "I guess I just got really bored with everything."

"Kitchen cleanser?"

"You can shoot it, but I cut it into my arm with an X-Acto knife."

Then she pulled one of her Chicago Cubs wristbands up and showed me this purple scar that was like an inch long and pretty deep.

"You can touch it," she said.

I ran a finger across it, and it thrilled me for some reason.

"Kiss it," she then said, so that's what I did.

"There," she said, and pulled the wristband back up.

"How did you wind up here?" I asked.

"They thought I might be schizophrenic, but they tested me and I'm not," she said. "So Burnstone Grove was the next option. My parents are basically shitheads who don't want to deal."

I will go into more detail about the events surrounding my loss of virginity later, but I am getting too excited and I think I should probably return to what happened after I fell asleep in that alley.

Which was that I woke up naked.

I'd been feasted on pretty ferociously by mosquitoes and it felt like my whole body itched. The weird thing was that I was still wearing my Red Wing boots, which were moist with my own vomit.

I had fallen asleep in that alley and I was sort of sprawled out on my stomach. I rolled over and looked up. My clothes were hanging from the fire escape, like twenty feet in the air. I have no idea how they got there. I looked in my dad's Marine Corps bag for a pair of underwear. Inside there was a bottle of Robitussin and an almost-empty pack of cigarettes and nothing else.

I swallowed.

My mouth tasted like gravel.

I had about four headaches going at once.

I grabbed my dad's Marine Corps bag and pushed on.

You'd be surprised how far you can walk into the more commercial sections of downtown Foote while completely nude. It might have been 6:30 A.M.

I fished a copy of the *Foote Daily Bugle* out of a trash can. I wrapped it around my waist. The *Foote Daily Bugle* is actually salmon-colored, which isn't bad fashion when you're using newspapers as clothes.

I tried lighting a cigarette, but it was soaked with Robitussin and it wouldn't burn.

My *Foote Daily Bugle* miniskirt crackled with each step. A fifth headache started materializing. I found myself walking toward my dad's electronics shop. It was only about six blocks away, and my legs were just sort of taking me there. At this point I had pretty much decided that I was going to kill myself. Why I chose my dad's shop for this, I don't know. I didn't even know how I was going to do it, to tell you the truth—maybe I would pummel my head with an antique cash register or electrocute myself with an old toaster oven or something. I guess I just wanted everything to end, and that's all I could think about while I was heading there. I told you before how I'm part Blue Grouper. Well, this is where that part reared its ugly head.

The sky was still pretty dark and the heat had totally lifted. I was shivering so much it was making it hard to walk.

When I reached the shop, the lights were off and the OPEN sign hadn't yet been turned around. They'd done something weird to the door. It looked like the paint had been totally sanded off of it.

Through the window, I was surprised to see Lyman Singer working the books at the counter. It was way too early for anyone to be up and working.

I knocked on the door. Lyman Singer's eyes were closed. For a moment I thought he was praying. When I knocked again, he opened his eyes and made this face. I know I was probably the last person in the world he wanted to see. And in my condition it must have been at least a little shocking for him. He studied his watch and squeezed around the counter and opened the door.

"Is that you, Steven?" he asked. There was a pencil fisted in his hand.

I was like, "Yeah, it's me."

"Are you okay?"

What I wanted to do was sit down and ask him for a drink of water, but for some reason, even though she was already dead, I felt the need to say, "My mom had this dream about Welton."

"Oh," he responded politely.

"He was at the circus, and his pants kept falling down."

Lyman Singer just kept staring at me and holding on to that pencil.

I said, "That's pretty funny, right?"

"Sure," he answered. "That is quite funny."

His head was bald and huge. I'd never noticed how big it was before.

"You're wearing the newspaper, Steven," he said. "And your poor chest is bleeding," he added, still holding the pencil. "What happened?"

I started feeling like I was going to fall. I had to lean against the counter.

"Things have been a little weird lately," I tried to explain. The words came out slow and they felt huge in my mouth.

"Here," he said, "sit down."

"No thanks," I said.

I felt like if I just kept standing, things would somehow work themselves out.

The shop smelled like glue, and it was making my stomach knot up. I didn't sit. I just sort of kept leaning on the counter.

"Why are you here so early?" I asked.

"I've been pulling a lot of double duty since your mom got sick," he explained. "Your dad's needed some time to deal with things at home."

"Yeah," I said, "things at home pretty much suck."

"Well," he said, "grief does strange things to all of us, Steven." His hands were tense and hairy. I thought the pencil was going to snap. "I'm just staying here till we get confirmation that the new alarm system is functioning. I have an old cot set up in the office. Here, take my shirt," he said, slipping out of this light-blue cotton pullover. It had a collar and there was an alligator on it. There were patches of hair all over his stomach and shoulders, and he had these totally flabby, womanish-looking chest muscles.

"Thanks," I said, pulling his shirt over my head. It smelled like after-shave and avocados.

"Let me see if I have an extra pair of trousers back

232

in the office," he offered, disappearing into the small room on the other side of the counter.

I could hear him sorting though some boxes in the office. I scanned the shop. They had already started to reorganize. There were new shelves, and the floor had been polished. I could just see my dad operating one of those rented oscillating machines, the marble floor getting all buffed and slippery, Lyman Singer erecting the new shelves, measuring the Sheetrock, getting fancy with those plastic dry-wall anchors, using the power drill.

I almost fell again, but I continued to use the counter.

Lyman Singer returned with a pair of these totally satin, parachute-looking slacks things. They were so red they practically laughed.

"You're more than welcome to use them," he said, offering the pants. "They're part of my old clown costume. I used to do these kids' shows. . . ."

I stepped out of my boots, let my *Foote Daily Bugle* miniskirt fall to the floor, and started to slip into the clown pants.

We stared at each other for a moment. My permanent marker black bush looked like some weird birthmark I'd never be able to get rid of. You could hear the air conditioner going back in the office.

"I'm so sorry about your mother, Steven," Lyman

Singer said. "I didn't get a chance to express my condolences at the memorial."

But I didn't want things to get all weird so I was like, "My dad been by?"

"He was here last night," he said. "He actually left something for you. In case you were to stop in."

"What is it?" I asked.

Lyman Singer pushed buttons on the old-fashioned cash register. It chimed and rattled, and after he struck its side a few times, the drawer flew open. He reached under the tray and produced an envelope. I could see my name on it. Well, it wasn't my name, really.

It said:

Son

Lyman handed it to me and I tore it open. Inside was a crisp one-hundred-dollar bill. Ben Franklin's face staring back at me again. Underneath the cash was a note. It read:

Steve,
    Use the money for whatever
you need.
    Dad

Also included was a longer letter. I didn't bother with that and stuffed it back in the envelope. I shoved the cash into the pocket of my clown pants and put the envelope in my dad's Marine Corps bag.

"I'm sorry about the shop," I said to Lyman Singer.

"Steve," he replied, "what's done is done. I understand you've been through a lot. Your whole family has. What you did is forgivable. *I* forgive you. Your father forgives you. I'm sure God forgives you."

"God's just bored," is what I said for some reason.

Then I almost fell again, but I played it off pretty well and caught my balance.

"You should really call your father," Lyman Singer continued. "One doesn't want to live in regret. An intelligent, sensitive young man like you."

"He might as well be dead, too," I said.

"Steven, he's your *father*."

I said, "If you see him, tell him I say hey."

"Life goes on, Steve," he added. "You need to stop punishing yourself and try connecting with those who care about you."

I exited the shop with my dad's Marine Corps bag. My clown pants were light and satiny. When the new door closed behind me, it made a loud click.

24

The Foote sky was pretty gray that morning. There was no wind and the streets seemed eerily calm. It usually gets that way before tornados. The thought didn't put me much at ease.

I entered the Dunkin' Donuts on Culvert Street. A radio was playing easy-listening rock. Coffee was brewing. There was a sign over the cash register that said that Dunkin' Donuts possessed the best coffee in the world. A man was doing stuff behind the counter. He had a mustache and he wore a smock. He was arranging hundreds of colored donuts and sort of humming along to some totally overly inspiring Whitney Houston song.

The fluorescent light was harsh, and it made my whole face hot. My clown pants billowed about my legs, and I knew in my heart that I looked incredibly stupid. Lyman Singer's baby-blue golf shirt was sticking to my skin, and little flowers of blood were sort of bleeding through from where I had been raking away at all my mosquito bites. My Red Wings stank of sweat and vomit, and I was having a problem telling whether or not I could feel my shin anymore. The air conditioning was so cold that it somehow made everything feel like it didn't matter, even more than just hours before.

The man behind the counter finished arranging a row of these things that looked like the glazed anuses of blond orangutans. He turned. He eyed me with a surprising lack of suspicion.

"Can I help you?" he asked.

"Um, sure," I said. "I'd like . . ."

I could feel something running out of my stomach. It was sort of intense. It actually felt like something was *scurrying* out of me.

"Yes?" the man said.

Whatever it was ran up my chest and sort of got stuck in my throat. My ears felt suddenly missing, like they'd been twisted off or something.

"Would you like another minute?" the man asked.

"No," I said, "I—"

And then, just like that, my mouth was full of blood. The taste of it was all warm and metallic. The man stared at me with a pretty suspicious look all of a sudden. I was probably making some horrible, tortured face.

"Are you okay, son?" he asked.

I shook my head.

Then he actually leaned toward me, and I made a strange gurgling noise that sounded more like something a car would produce, and vomited on him. It was mostly blood. There was suddenly this like gross, extra-large pink tulip running down his white Dunkin' Donuts smock.

He rushed around to the other side of the counter and attempted to help me. I remember that his nametag said BILL.

"Take it easy now," he said, trying to keep me from falling. "Steady as she goes."

It felt like the laws of gravity had suddenly changed pretty intensely. Bill led me to a booth and I sat, still managing to hold on to my dad's Marine Corps bag. The table was cold and clean, and I was suddenly keenly aware that my teeth were chattering.

"I got a hundred bucks, I got a hundred b-b-bucks," is all I could say for some reason.

"No need to worry about money," Bill said. "Stay right there. I'm going to call the hospital, okay?"

I nodded.

Then he disappeared.

My tongue felt all contorted and tight, and my heart was beating so hard I could almost taste it in my mouth.

Bill was talking to medical officials on the phone.

"Yeah, a lot of blood," he was saying. "Orally, yes. Through his mouth. . . . Just some kid off the street. . . . No, I don't think he's homeless. He looks pretty beat up."

I reached into that envelope that my dad had left for me at the electronics shop. I removed the folded piece of paper. It was handwritten in blue ink, and the cursive was sort of faint and childish-looking. My teeth were still chattering like crazy, and I couldn't keep my hands from shaking. I did my best to flatten the letter on the table.

It read:

Remember Me

Remember me, please. An ordinary woman with a good heart. A woman who loved her children and took great pride in them. Remember me—I was the big sister, the second mom, the confidant who'd always listen to a problem and try to be helpful. Remember me—a plain Jane who wore glasses and had irregular skin and large hands that could comfort. Remember that I was a great nurse who treated everyone with the same compassion. Remember that I wanted our family to be close but that I died without that happening and I felt sad about it.

To my sister, Ricky: Don't forget all those phone calls when we'd crack up laughing over anything and everything and that you were a great comfort to me when things got bad.

To Chris and Dot: I'll take with me the memories of your help and concern. You lived so far away, yet cared so much.

To my two boys: Remember that I loved you both with my whole heart and though I was far from the perfect mom, I did the best I knew how. Welton, have faith that your back will heal and that you will one day again play basketball. Steven Jacob, remember that I loved you—my "white knight"—and would have done anything to stay with you. I think you are the smartest person I know, my sweet boy.

Richard, my love, remember to enjoy life. I always felt you were the brave and strong one. I admired you so much.

Remember that I loved books, classical music,
patchwork quilts, my bed, sunshine, spring,
Charles Wysocki's art, and a good laugh.

The Moon will rise
The Sun will set
Please do not forget . . .

Mary Lee Nugent

I folded the piece of paper and put it back in the
envelope.

Then I stood. But that was too hard, so I sat.

I had my money. And I had my dad's Marine
Corps bag.

I stood again.

For some reason I counted to four. One, two, and
three came out with relative ease. But four was like
some gastrointestinal freight train. My body made a
sound like an elephant burping and then I hit the floor.

Which was covered with hard, white tiles.

I could smell cleaning products.

A sour mop. Fresh doughnuts.

Then everything went red.

Easy-listening rock was on the radio.

25

Sleep was gigantic and soft.

I dreamed of a fast-food community dinner. The dream took place at the McDonald's by the civic center. June was there. Mary Mills was there. My mom and dad were there, too. The lights over the hamburger grills were all screwed up, and bugs were sort of swarming everywhere. My community service supervisor—that guy Jerry Willems I was telling you about—was standing on a ladder trying to change a tray of fluorescent tubes.

June took our order. She was smoking my last Camel Light and it looked so good I wanted to snatch it out of her mouth, but my hands were too heavy.

The dining area was filled with cops and teachers and gym coaches. The gym coaches were trying to organize a restaurant-wide Presidential Physical Fitness Test. There would be a standing broad jump. There would be pull-ups. There would be sit-ups and an improvised shuttle run involving condiments and Special Sauce.

I tried to sneak away. They captured me, though, and made me do the standing broad jump, but my feet were too heavy and I couldn't even jump a foot.

"Not very promising, Nugent," they said. "Not very promising."

In the middle of the dining area, there was this nude, twelve-foot maniac guy. His nudity was pretty alarming. He was standing on top of a table screaming, *"Drop the chalupa! Drop the chalupa!"* but everyone was ignoring him.

I eventually escaped and took my food outside to the picnic tables. Mary Mills and my mom were sitting in each others' laps, all playful and girlish. My dad kept announcing that he couldn't find his car keys.

An alien robot was there, too. He materialized right out of the garbage. He was taller than the maniac, and he was holding a huge tulip. He was made of metal, but he had this totally human erection. I had the feeling that the robot's erection was *my* erection, but when I looked down my pants, there was a small compact disc player. A Sony with G-Protection. I opened the lid, but it was empty.

At first I thought Welton was the alien robot, but toward the end of the dream, I realized that it was actually me. And when I finally made this connection, it became like code-red crucial that I exchange my compact disc player penis for the robot's erection. Why this was code-red crucial, I have no idea, but it felt like everything totally depended on it.

I woke to a nurse feeding a tube into my right arm. She was so white she appeared to be lit from within. Her arms were flabby and her hands smelled like lotion and her mouth was so small it seemed sewn shut. I prayed she wouldn't speak.

She was sliding the needle under my skin. My arm seemed dead. It looked like meat from the butcher's.

The IV needle was cold, and I couldn't see out of my right eye. This biological fact registered much later than it should have. Things to the right just weren't making their way into my field of vision. My left eye told me that there was a TV, an empty bed beside mine, and this totally monstrous rubberized plant that looked so highly advanced I feared it would hop down off the windowsill and ambush me.

There were two vertical slats set up on either side of my neck, positioned at the ears, apparently to keep my head from moving.

A pain materialized. It was that kind of pain that makes it hard to breathe. I located it above my neck, then in my head, then, more specifically, in my right eye. Everything on the right side of my body sort of throbbed, and I was afraid to move.

I felt my right hand rising toward my face.

"Don't touch now," the nurse said.

"Where am I?" I asked.

"You're in the intensive care unit of the ophthalmology ward at Medical Associates."

I said, "What happened?"

My voice sounded like it had been taken out and put back in.

"Well, from what I hear, you put your own thumb through your right eye. You have a shield over it. The doctor will be able to give you details."

It felt like there was half of a football helmet totally welded over the right side of my face.

"How do you feel?" she asked.

"I don't know," I said. "Not so good."

"This'll help," she said, fastening a strip of tape over my now-inserted IV needle.

"What is it?"

"Well, this is a narcotic that will make you feel better and help you relax."

"What kind of narcotic?"

"Morphine."

I said, "Whoa."

"It should kick in in a few minutes. The fluid fed

into your left hand is a rehydrating electrolyte. You were terribly dehydrated, Steven. Your system was practically poisoned with antihistamines."

"How did you know my name?" I asked.

"We found your school ID in your bag. Your brother and father were here earlier, but you were still out cold. They'll be back. The doctor will be by later this afternoon to check on you. Try not to move. We need to keep your venous pressure to a minimum."

Then I asked her what venous pressure was, because I'd thought she said penis at first, and she explained that it was the pressure in your veins and that the main concern was to keep my optic nerve pumping so things wouldn't get "shut down," as she described it.

"The less you move your head around, the better," she warned. "Try not to sneeze or laugh or cough. And if you need to move your bowels, just relax and let yourself go. You've been fitted with a diaper."

"I'm wearing a diaper?" I asked.

"Don't be embarrassed."

She dabbed a cotton ball full of alcohol over the small hole she had just made in me. It was cold and stayed that way for like ten minutes.

When she left, this totally weird sadness overwhelmed me.

246

Fluorescent lights sort of droned.

My bed smelled clean and sterile.

A TV loomed above me, all blank and omnipotent.

I almost started crying, but I made myself stop because of all that venous pressure business. And then my sadness was replaced by something much, much, much, much, much, much, much, more powerful: morphine.

I will say this:

With morphine there is no longing.

There is no hunger.

There is no need for sex or clothes or friendship.

There is only love.

The pain disappeared so fast I almost missed it.

I suddenly loved the smell of my bed. The TV was my best friend, the plant a sexless time-traveling monk sent to my room to bless me. Everything was right in the world. Even my thoughts turned suddenly clear and hopeful. I started setting goals. I would go to college! I would scale the holy ivy at some totally tweedish liberal-arts institution in the Northeast! I would wear khakis and penny loafers and freshly laundered underwear! I would learn all there is to know about the history of this beautiful country and how things came to be! I would yearn for knowledge! I would flourish and expand! My body would fill out handsomely, and girls would find me interesting and entertaining! My pubic hair would finally grow in with fantastic, undulating curls! I would graduate with honors and work in a major city and my gabled New England home would have several rooms where my blond-haired, blue-eyed, fourteen-thousand-word-vocabulary children would play chess and read complicated novels! I would move beyond math and solve the mystery of bacteria! I would be awarded and anthologized! Busts of my likeness would be erected on all the great lawns! I would die in my eighties and leave behind a legacy of Nugent geniuses-to-be!

Then an elderly man was wheeled into my room. He was pretty lifeless-looking, and his head was covered with gauze. The staff attending his gurney huddled around and manipulated his chart and whispered truths and medical poetry. After a moment they pulled a curtain between us and exited. There were things beeping all around him.

This was not a man, my morphine mind told me. This was a beast of love sent to my room to radiate warmth and a healing holiness.

I suddenly had to go to the bathroom. This was okay. This was fine. My morphine mind told me that this was bliss, in fact. So I urinated warmly. And I defecated softly. I released my bowels and felt glad. I was highly entertained by this and I smiled throughout.

In the other bed, the elderly man moaned. It was a pretty intense moan. I imagined both of his eyes missing. Two enormous diamonds fitted into his sockets instead.

He moaned again and then added, "Nurse! Nurse! Oh, my God! Somebody help me! Nurse!"

Moments later my nurse entered the room.

"Yes, Mr. Johnson?" she asked calmly.

"Where are you?" he asked.

"I'm right beside you, Mr. Johnson. I'm right here. Are you in pain?"

"No, not pain, no. No pain."

"What can I do for you?" she asked.

"I want to know if I'm going to be able to see."

"The doctor said it was a successful operation, but we won't know what the actual outcome will be until we remove the bandages. You need to heal a bit before we can do that."

"I want to know now!"

"I know you do, Mr. Johnson, but we don't want any early, unwanted light to damage your eyes, do we?"

Mr. Johnson didn't respond. He breathed and sighed. He was really scared.

"Is that clear, Mr. Johnson?" the nurse asked. "Do you understand me, Mr. Johnson?"

He finally replied, "I understand you. Go away."

The nurse turned to leave and then it dawned on me.

"Nurse?" I asked.

"Yes, Steven?"

I said, "What about me?"

"What about you, Steven?"

"My right eye. Am I like blind?"

"It was a very serious puncture, Steven," the nurse said. "There's a strong chance that you've lost vision in your right eye."

26

I woke to the sound of a squealing gurney.

The morphine had worn off a bit and I came to feeling pretty sad and dislocated. My last conscious memory was talking to the doctor. Dr. Black was his name. He visited in the middle of the night. He was bald but had bushy eyebrows and hairy hands. His breath smelled like Certs and Tater Tots.

Dr. Black told me that I had this thing called a hyphema, an optical hemorrhage caused by a tear in the pupil. He used terms like "vitreous humor" and "aqueous humor," words that somehow sounded like they came from the sea.

In addition to his baldness and Certs-and-Tater-Tots breath, Dr. Black was an unusually tan man. He sort of looked like a professional golfer, now that I think about it.

He went on to tell me that there was an eighty-percent chance of me losing all sight in my right eye, and then he slowly powered my bed into a V-shape. It felt strange to sit up. The morphine had done something to gravity and other natural laws. I felt like I had been beaten and that things inside me had been removed, rearranged, and put back in.

"In a moment I'm going to need you to open that eye," Dr. Black said, suddenly producing this contraption that looked like a thing used to calculate the weight and quality of bat feces. He called it a "slit lamp" and told me that it was a device used to measure the pressure in my eyeball.

"I don't want you to be alarmed if you can't see anything. Your blindness is not necessarily permanent."

Necessarily? I thought.

When I opened my right eye, all that registered was a murderous sea of red. There were no outlines, nothing defining height or depth, only red and *redder* red. When I opened my good eye, the world bounced back into my brain with a fluorescent vengeance. Then I closed it, opened my bad eye, and everything went red again.

Dr. Black said it was red because the back of my eye was bleeding into my retina. For some reason I imagined my eye menstruating. Like my eye was having its first period or whatever.

He fitted my face into the slit lamp. There was a chin strap. There was a very white, very small spotlight.

There was a strange little metal nipple that he explained would have to "touch my eyeball" in order to obtain a proper pressure reading. The prospect of something touching my eye was pretty alarming, to say the least—especially something metal and nipple-shaped. Morphine or no morphine, I experienced what I can only describe as a brain scream. Terror and morphine do not mix. The morphine only relaxes the body, so that the terror can sink its monstrous talons deeper into your drug-calmed flesh. I prayed I wouldn't defecate in my pants while Dr. Black got his "pressure reading."

He told me to close my good eye and worked my bad eye open with his fingertips and said relaxing things like "This won't hurt a bit," and, "It'll be over before you know it." Things that basically make you clench up in anticipation of hypodermic needles or dental drills. The little white spotlight was drawn so close to my eye that I could feel the heat radiating from its tiny bulb. Moments later there was the faintest touch on my eyeball. It could have been a moth wing.

He repeated this three times. That was it, he said. That was all he needed.

Dr. Black said that soon he would start to administer what he called "healing drops" twice a day and that if the pressure was kept down, there would be a chance of regaining *some* of my vision. When asked what these healing drops were, he said they were optical steroids that would help the rupture repair itself. Like the nurse, he warned me not to move and encouraged me to use my diapers.

Then Dr. Black started to pack up his slit lamp.

"So how long will I be in here?" I asked. My throat was pretty dry and sore.

"Well, that all depends on your venous pressure," he said, redressing my patch. "If the readings increase, we may need to do surgery. If they go down on their own, then there's a good chance for recovery. This was your first reading and it's pretty high, so we'll get a better idea over the next few days.

"I've had hyphema patients who've had to stay in the hospital for weeks," he explained. "Others left after a few days. The eyeball is a mysterious organ. Some people respond better to this condition than others. The key is stillness. How's the pain?"

"Not so great."

"Well, use the morphine. We can only keep you on it for a few days at a time, so use it liberally."

Then he pressed the little button attached to my morphine cartridge and left in sort of a rush.

The second wave of sleep was beautiful and deep. Like mermaids leading me through warm, breathable water.

27

The next time I woke, my dad was sitting in a chair next to the bed. He had turned on the TV, and its light was making his face look sort of old and bloodless.

On QVC these two overly caffeinated guys were narrating sales pitches about the most important things ever to be invented by the human race: sports cards.

One of the guys, whose voice was being transmitted over what sounded like some totally fake phone line (he was probably speaking into a mike through a pair of pantyhose), kept saying that he was "stone cold dead serious."

"I am stone cold dead serious, ladies and gentlemen," he swore to us. "You will *not*! I repeat *not* find a Tiger Woods rookie card at a lower price ANYWHERE!!! You'd be a friggin' *idiot* not to take ad*van*tage . . ."

The camera would occasionally pan to his partner, who was actually handling the cards in a makeshift home studio. That guy looked like some kind of overly showered hitman posing as a Christian youth organizer.

He spoke with such passion and velocity, you would have thought he was powered not by blood and oxygen but by gasoline and other combustible fluids.

My dad was wearing an old red bowling shirt with his name embroidered on the chest in yellow cursive stitching. He'd finally changed out of that suit, thank God. It was the first time I'd seen him since I'd taken off. He looked pretty horrible. His hair appeared to be somehow fried. His stubble looked sort of rusty. He was really thin, too.

Those QVC guys were screaming at him to take the Tiger Woods rookie card for two payments of $450.

"Take the card! Take the card!" they screamed.

It was like they were punishing him.

Then my dad turned toward me. I could see him through the crust in my unpatched eye. He watched me with this totally pathetic look on his face, almost like he was starving or something.

After a moment he rose out of his chair and took a step toward me. I sealed my eye. I had no idea what he was planning to do, but I have to admit that I was sort of hoping that he would maybe put a hand on my shoulder or fluff my hair.

But what he did was lean over me and pick up the phone that was on the other side of my bed. His breath smelled all weird and soapy, like he had washed his own mouth out. I thought maybe he was shampooing with Crest and brushing his teeth with Irish Spring or something.

The dial tone sounded so far away it made me feel like I was in another country.

My dad punched in a number. It took him so long the touch-tones practically echoed. A receptionist's voice came on the line like a faint bee buzzing. She said, "Hello," or, "Good evening," or whatever scripted greeting she was forced to recite, and then in a tired, dehydrated tenor my dad told her that he wanted to purchase the Tiger Woods rookie card for two payments of $450. After agreeing with the woman on the other end of the phone a few times, he recited his credit card number from memory.

All sixteen digits, plus the expiration date.

Another time I woke and Welton was sitting in the same chair. It was pulled very close to my bed and his forehead was sort of resting on my mattress. I had no idea what time it was.

After a minute I realized that I had been making a fist with my morphine hand. It felt cold and strange. When I lifted it to feel the crown of Welton's head, I could see that he had removed my morphine IV and inserted it into the webbing between the index and middle finger of his right hand.

You hear about how brothers take cross-country road trips or camp in national forests. Well, this was our first Brothers Nugent journey. My hand eventually did find its way through the velveteen perfection of his hair, and when he looked up, we understood something so pure that it defies words, something that perhaps only birds know, birds or like deer or caribou, or other mammals that can leap and at times achieve temporary flight.

We eventually fell into a kind of half-dreamed sleep, my hand planted on his head, his thumb depressing the little button attached to my morphine toy.

When security came for him, his body was limp and lifeless. I remember his delirious laughter as he was ushered through the door. It was one of the goofiest laughs I've ever heard.

On the eighth day, they finally let me out of bed. The nurse suggested that I use the wall for balance. At the end of the hall, there was an upright scale. For some reason I felt the need to weigh myself. As I already told you, I'm skinny. There is no way around this biological fact. Sopping wet I'm around 145 pounds. The scale at Medical Associates read 127 pounds. At six three, that basically made me a human pipe cleaner. Granted, since my homelessness I hadn't been exactly eating three square meals, and in the hospital I had only ingested a few bowls of green Jell-O and whatever rehydrating fluids they had been pumping into me. I could feel my ribs through my pajamas. I felt somehow made of wood. Like some sort of weird totem created by fitness professionals to illustrate the tragedy of adolescence, a life-size puppet to be kept behind the health-class movie projector and only taken out after children had certain permission slips signed by their parents.

I was totally desperate for a cigarette.

After weighing myself, I started wandering. Following the nurse's orders I did use the wall for balance, and it was a pretty good idea, as my legs were weak and my skull felt too heavy for my neck. I got a head rush and sort of stumbled into this little kid's room. He was lying on his back, on top of the covers, wearing Chicago Cubs pajamas and hugging this big black first baseman's mitt. I stood in the doorway and watched him for a minute. There was a bandage around his head, so much gauze you couldn't even see his hair. His skin looked all weird and bluish. For a moment I thought he was dead.

"Are you the guy who's s'posed to read to me?" he asked. His voice was surprisingly strong and clear.

I said, "I was just sort of walking around."

"You're a patient?"

"Yeah," I said. "I'm a patient."

"Which room?"

"I don't know the number," I said. "The one with the weird plant."

"Oh, that's Grover," he said.

I went, "Grover?"

"I had that room a few times last month. The nurse asked me to name the plant."

I was like, "Cool name," and continued hovering in the doorway.

There was a pretty intense sadness in this room, a feeling that no one ever visited, like it had been lost through a black hole in the hospital and the only way to be admitted back into the ranks of the afflicted was by solving some sort of impossible medical riddle.

His chart hung off the end of his bed all sad and metallic, like a thing placed there not to mark his progress but rather to record his slow, deliberate inching toward death.

He said, "If you're looking for a cigarette, you should ask the lady at the front desk."

His insight hit me in the knees like an aluminum baseball bat. I felt myself teeter a bit.

I was like, "How did you know I was looking for a cigarette?"

"I've already had three smokers in here today."

The kid yawned and adjusted the mitt on his chest.

"So you're not the reader?" he asked.

"No," I said. "I'm not."

"The last guy smelled like onions. He kept trying to read that stupid book about the elephant."

"Babar?"

"Yeah, Babar," he said. "So boring."

The kid moved the mitt over his face and in this totally sophisticated FM radio voice said, "Some experts from Yellowstone National Park believe that if a man sits still enough in the presence of a bear, the bear will speak great unknown truths to him."

I said, "Whoa."

He put the mitt back on his chest and went, "That was on the Discovery Channel earlier. I can't watch it but I can listen. Wanna watch Discovery Channel with me? They're s'posed to be doing this thing on the great hermit penguins of the Arctic."

"No thanks," I said. "I should get back to my room. I'm not used to being on my feet."

And this was true. I could feel my weakness spreading.

"Sit down," the kid said. "I don't bite."

I sat on a chair.

We were quiet for a moment.

"So what are you in here for?" I asked.

"A vessel broke in my brain."

I went, "Like a blood vessel?"

"Yeah, a blood vessel. A few months ago, I started knocking my head against the wall. They made me wear a football helmet. Since the medication, I haven't been hitting things with my head, but I can't see sometimes and I have to come in every few weeks. Sometimes they do stuff to my brain."

"Like what?"

"They go in my head and look around. They shaved all my hair off last time."

"So you're like bald?"

"Uh-huh. Wanna feel it?"

I went, "No thanks," and felt my own head instead. It was cold and stubbly.

I asked, "Can you see now?"

"Not too good. Mostly shadows. I saw one of the orderlies earlier. He had big ears. The nurse said I'll prolly be able to see more stuff tomorrow. What about you? What are you in here for?"

"Um, I sort of punctured my eye."

"Ow."

"Yeah."

"So you're just walking the halls?" he asked.

I was like, "Yeah. They haven't let me move for like a week. I've been totally cooped up."

"The venous pressure thing, huh?"

"Yeah. You too?"

"I'm not supposed to be moving now, but I move, see?" he said, suddenly standing in the middle of his bed. He was so small he looked ceramic, like one of those Nativity statues they set in front of churches. He turned a full circle and sat back down.

"Sometimes I even get out of bed," he added.

"You're beating the system," I offered. "How old are you?"

"Seven and a half. I'll be eight on St. Patrick's Day. What about you?"

"Sixteen. I'll be seventeen in November."

He said, "You're tall, aren't you?"

"How can you tell?"

"Your voice."

I said, "My voice isn't deep."

"It's not deep but it's tall. Are you a seven-footer?"

"I'm a little over six three."

"Oh," he said. "My dad died last week."

It came out just like that. He could have said his dad weighed seventy-seven pounds or he liked blue cheese salad dressing. It was a harmless biographical fact.

I was like, "How'd he die?"

"He had lowkemia. He was bald, too, but he wore this wig that made him look like Grover Cleveland. At least that's what my mom said."

I swallowed.

I breathed.

I said, "Sorry. Are you like sad?"

"No," he said. "But my sister is. And so is my cat."

"What's your cat's name?"

"Leroy."

"Cool name. What kind of cat is he?"

"Black. He gets in trouble 'cause he jumps on the curtains. My mom took his claws off."

"Does your mom visit you here?"

"She's down in the cafeteria."

I pictured his mom down in the cafeteria, eating macaroni and cheese out of those weird Styrofoam containers.

"My sister's comin' by later, too," he said. "She promised me Chicken McNuggets. They're good with peanut butter."

"They are?"

"Yeah. Stick around. You can try it."

I said, "I should get going. They'll probably freak out if they don't see me back in my room."

Then the kid raised the baseball mitt to his face and did it again.

This time he said, "The Alaskan polar bear is one of the great Arctic nomads. She dines on fish and the occasional sea lion. Those who cross her path better have a dogsled nearby or they might wind up as the evening's main course. Just ask this pesky otter."

I said, "That's pretty impressive."

"I can do this thing on the caribou, too," he said, lowering the baseball mitt. "But I'll save that for next time."

Then we were quiet. I could hear things moving down the corridor. Gurneys and wheelchairs and monitors.

"So when are you getting out of here?" I asked.

"As soon as my sight comes back. Maybe tonight, maybe tomorrow. Sometimes it takes a few days. The lady from Children's Services wants to teach me Braille. Just in case I don't get it back this time."

For some reason, thinking of him blind made me want to sit on the floor, so that's what I did.

But after a second my head started feeling really heavy. So I pushed myself off the floor and sat back in the chair.

"So you play baseball?" I asked.

"I used to," he replied.

"What position?"

"Center field."

"Good arm?"

"It's okay. I can make it back to the infield."

"Pretty impressive. Can you hit?"

"I was starting to figure it out. The bat's pretty heavy, though. You don't play, do you?"

"No."

"You don't like sports," he said with a slight smile.

"How do you know I don't like sports?"

"I can just tell."

I said, "You're pretty smart, huh?"

"Your voice gives it away. Why don't you like sports?"

"I don't know."

"Your voice says you don't like much of anything."

I said, "That's so not true. I like stuff."

"What do you like?"

"Um, I like girls. And cigarettes. And I totally worship greyhounds."

I wanted to say morphine, too, but that would have made me more of a criminal than I already was.

"Dogs are better than people," he said.

"I'll agree with that."

"When I come back, I want to be a schnauzer."

I said, "Come back from where?"

"The dead. We all get reincarnated. My aunt Francine has a schnauzer. His name is Mister Big Stuff and he eats spaghetti."

I laughed and it made my lungs ache. I tried not to cough in fear of that whole venous pressure business.

The kid sort of turned to me. The flesh over his eyes looked gray and thin.

"So what are you good at?" he asked.

I said, "I don't know. Nothing really."

"You gotta be good at *somethin'*."

"I'm okay at math, I guess."

"You are?"

"Sort of. I'm actually the number two Mathlete at my school."

"What's twelve times twelve?"

"A hundred and forty-four."

"Six times six."

"Thirty-six."

"One-third of sixty-six."

"Twenty-two."

He said, "You *are* good at math."

"Thanks," I said.

"Wanna sign my glove?"

"Um. Sure."

"There's a marker in the thumb slot."

I walked over to him and took the glove. There were signatures all over it. Little pictures of things, too, like smiley faces and flowers and a baseball with bumblebee wings.

I signed my name and handed it back.

He pulled the mitt close to his face and tried to read it and then he touched the area I signed and went, "What's your name?"

"Steve," I said.

"Steve what?"

"Steve Nugent. They call me White Steve."

"How come?"

"Because I'm really white."

"I found a white corn snake once. They said it was an alpine."

"Do you mean albino?" I said.

"I mean *albino,*" he echoed, correcting himself and laughing a little. "My mom made me give it away 'cause I kept puttin' it in the bathtub."

I laughed again and so did he.

I said, "What's *your* name?"

"Steve."

"Really?"

"Yep."

"Steven with a *v* or a *ph*?"

"A *v*."

I was like, "We're both Steves!"

"Yep."

"That's pretty cool, right?!"

Then he went, "Steve squared," and that's when I started crying. I have no idea why but I couldn't stop. The kid just sat there and listened.

"Sorry," I said, wiping my unshielded eye. My tears were hot and they stank like medicine.

"It's okay," he said. "Crying's like rain. It makes the grass grow in your soul. That's what my mom says." Then he very classily changed the subject and went, "Even in the horizontal mountains of Ojai, the shifty mountain lion is a force to be reckoned with. If you cross its path, don't turn around or you may find one clinging to your back."

For that one he didn't use the glove. But he still assumed the sophisticated FM radio voice.

"I made that one up," he said.

"You're pretty good."

"Penguins in twenty minutes."

"I better get back to my room."

"Okay."

"Take it easy."

"You too."

I hovered at the door for a second. We didn't say anything. He hardly moved in the bed. He was above things somehow. He was somewhere else, flying with butterflies and other weightless, pollen-dusted creatures. When I think about it now, part of me believes that I could have stayed in that doorway forever. It may have been the closest thing to a good feeling I'd had since I kicked in all those TVs, not counting the morphine, of course.

For some reason I felt sentimental and went, "Sorry about your dad." My voice bounced around the silent room for a moment and then I left.

In the hallway, my hospital pants made little whispery noises. Other half-blind patients were searching for the wall like me: old men, children, middle-aged women with heads covered with gauze.

When I finally got back to my room, I was exhausted and happy to return to bed. There was no more morphine, but that was probably good; otherwise I'd probably be a full-fledged Red Grouper by now.

I woke up in the middle of the night and walked into the bathroom. I removed my diaper and urinated in the toilet for the first time. To urinate standing up somehow made me feel like a regular person again.

In the mirror, my reflection was almost yellow. Man, those fluorescent hospital lights can make you pretty ugly. My lips were thin and blue. My ears looked somehow manually attached, like they were bought at some weird anatomical hardware store and screw-gunned to the sides of my head.

The medical tape holding my eye shield was loose, and I couldn't help taking a look.

Dr. Black had warned me the last time he had taken a pressure reading. "You might not like what you see," he said, packing up his slit lamp. "I wouldn't be tempted to peek just yet."

He said that the damage had caused some atrophy in the muscles around my eye and it might be pretty scary. He said it was "looking small" but assured me that in time it would return to its original shape.

When I removed the metal shield, my left eye told me that its partner had been replaced by a small, puck-ering anus, a thing plucked from the ass of a flying rodent or some totally emaciated bullfrog.

My knees started to go, but I leaned against the sink. I eventually reaffixed the shield and tried to erase the image from my mind.

I couldn't go back to bed so I walked out into the hall, where a few orderlies were mopping the floor.

My legs felt pretty wobbly.

"Can I help you, Steve?" the nurse on duty asked.

"I just wanted to walk around a little," I said.

"Be sure to use the wall," she replied, and returned to her computer.

I found myself back in front of that little kid Steve's room. He was still lying there, his baseball mitt resting on his chest. The light was off, and someone had brought him a poster of Sammy Sosa and taped it to the wall opposite his bed. Sammy was wearing a Cubs away jersey and smiling like his life depended on it.

I took a step into the room. Steve was sleeping pretty hard.

"My mom died," I said. I had no idea that was going to come out of my mouth, but it did. I sort of waited for him to respond, but he didn't. "She was a pediatric nurse," I continued. "She helped little kids. She used to *do* this thing," I remember hearing myself saying. "She'd try to look Chinese. She'd like squint her eyes and make her teeth look all bucked out or whatever and then she'd say, 'Pass the chop suey, Louie.' It was totally racist but she didn't mean it to be." Then I said it to him, I said, "Pass the chop suey, Louie. Pass the chop suey . . ."

But that little kid Steve wouldn't budge. Perhaps he had left his body and was roaming some unknown corridor where other kids were hiding from diseases or tumors or the ICU boogeyman.

"She had breast cancer," I added. "And she died."

Then the on-duty nurse was suddenly behind me. She said something but it didn't register. All I remember is that her voice was kind and gentle and sort of tired.

She moved me away and closed the door to Steve's room. Was this supposed to mean that *he* had died, too?

I sat on the floor.

It was hard and cold.

I could feel this totally thick sort of *anguishy* feeling taking over my body that has never quite left.

28

When Shannon Lynch left this afternoon, he gave me all the coins he used to stick up his nose. He also gave me that Sam Shepard play, *Buried Child*.

"Here," he said.

"Thanks," I said back.

Then he sort of pinched my cheek, which I thought was pretty weird, but I have to say that I'm glad he didn't try to kiss me again. He gave me his phone number at that place in Lake Geneva.

"Call me," he said.

"I will," I said, and I honestly plan on doing that.

"You should talk to your dad," he said when we were in front of the main building.

I sort of half nodded and told him to take care of himself.

It's sort of odd that he said that thing about talking to my dad, because we really never talked about that situation, but Shannon Lynch is obviously pretty perceptive about things.

Then he got into this white Burnstone Grove van and they pulled away through the front gate.

I felt sad when he left and I hope we stay in touch.

So back to the story part. . . .

The story part the story part the story part the story . . .

At some point my aunt Ricky moved in with us. I have this theory that certain members of your extended family are up above the clouds hovering in a radio-controlled fleet of hot-air balloons, and when a parent dies, some official representing the Office of the Great Family Tree or whatever steers them down from the sky so they can descend on your life and be totally annoying.

Aunt Ricky is a former grammar-school teacher and when she speaks to you, it's like she's about to walk you step-by-step through a series of instructional flash cards.

"Steven, honey," she said to me while attempting to salvage the crusted galaxy of dirty dishes in the sink, "I'm only here till you guys get back on your feet."

She stopped washing dishes for a moment and adjusted the small wooden crucifix hanging outside her blouse.

"It's only temporary," she continued, "and I don't want you to think for even a *minute* that I'm trying to replace your mother."

I didn't respond.

I hadn't said one word since I had been home, and I preferred it that way.

Aunt Ricky would say things like, "Don't pick at your shield, now."

And, "You're very lucky to have gotten your sight back, Steven. You should thank Jesus."

It was true. By some small miracle, I had gotten all my sight back.

In the kitchen light, Aunt Ricky's skin had this totally industrial, extra-strength quality. When she walked more than three steps, it took so much effort you couldn't help but anticipate some weird coronary disaster.

I'm convinced that her obsession with Jesus was far more romantic than spiritual. I think she was actually *attracted* to him. I sincerely thought that one day while out on a grocery run, she would find some skinny, bearded, out-of-work Foote guy on the side of the road and, convinced that he was our anorectic Son of God, rescue him and head for some unincorporated Christian town in the middle of Illinois with a bingo hall and lots of roadside crucifixes, never to return.

Aunt Ricky's deceased husband, Uncle Mike, even looked a little like Jesus, I'm not kidding, or at least he looked like one of his apostles. After the Marines,

Uncle Mike worked for the telephone company and fell out of one of those hydraulically lifted buckets and landed on his head and died of a broken neck. Since then, pretty much all Aunt Ricky does is accumulate garage-sale crucifixes and sleep with her collection of vintage rosaries.

Between Aunt Ricky's obsession with Jesus, my dad's life in front of the TV, and Welton's quiet, drug-induced romance with Sims and PlayStation II, I didn't have much in common with anyone in my house.

Aunt Ricky had been hard at work restoring the house to the way it was before my mom died. The living-room carpet had been vacuumed and treated with some totally floral-smelling powder. My dad's *TV Guide* epidemic had been arranged in bright, perpendicular stacks. The windows sparkled. The sofa had been cleaned and sealed with so much Scotchgard you could practically smell the fumes all the way from the front yard. Even the TV looked new, but it had merely been cleaned. And there were plants on the windowsills!

In the kitchen the floor gleamed and the counter-tops shone.

My second day back from the hospital, Aunt Ricky came into my room and said, "I want to read this to you, Steven." She spoke to me as if she was leading a troupe of Cub Scouts away from a bed of poison ivy. I was sitting at my desk, sort of just staring out the window. "It's something from your mother's journal," she continued. "She gave it to one of her hospice nurses before she passed."

And yes, Aunt Ricky preferred to use that word *passed,* like my mom was a *rowboat* or a patch of *bad weather* or something. Then she sat down at the foot of my bed, produced a piece of folded paper, cleared her throat, and read the following:

> I'm grateful for each day. Every morning
> when my alarm goes off, I'm happy to be able
> to stretch my legs out, give my dog a pat, and
> thank God for another day. My favorite days
> are those when the sun streams through my
> lace curtains, but I even like the sound of rain
> pattering on my window or the wind moving
> the trees against the side of the house. It is
> morning that gives me hope.

While she read it, I sort of left my body. The world outside the Nugent home was damp and cold. September was well upon us, and the trees along our street were all twisted like they had arthritis or something. Dogs barked and leaves whipped around yards in mini-tornadoes. Junior-high kids were driving BMX bikes and screeching down my street on their older brothers' skateboards. Soon they would be wearing Halloween costumes and all would be good in the world of East Foote.

"Do you have any thoughts about that, Steven?" Aunt Ricky asked, sort of wiping her cheeks. "About what I just read?"

"No," I said.

She just sort of sat there, nervously scratching these huge pink streaks into her forearms. She had eczema, and it was pretty gross. Certain humans are built to suffer, and living with my aunt Ricky convinced me of this fact. Besides being horribly overweight, she possessed bad skin, arthritic hips, several gray teeth, a lazy eye, a trick knee, varicose veins, and thinning, dyed orange hair.

"I understand your reticence, Steven," she continued. "If you want to talk about things, just let me know. I'm here for you."

Then she began the depressing four-part move of rocking at the foot of my bed to gain the momentum to lift her mass in an Atlas-like rebellion against gravity. She got pretty out of breath doing it, too. Then she sort of brushed off her nylon sweatpants and waddled into the kitchen, where I could hear her doing the dishes for like an hour. It was weird, too, because there were hardly any dishes *to* do. I think Aunt Ricky did them over and over sometimes just because she didn't know what else to do with her time.

The reason I can quote my mom's journal entry so well is because my aunt Ricky left it on my bed and I still have it.

That same night I woke with a start.

My bed felt all hard and wooden, like I was sleeping in a canoe or a floating coffin or something. I rose. I had this weird feeling that my room wasn't my room anymore. I can't quite explain why. It was almost like it was being prepared for some other kid or something. It was too clean. It smelled too fresh.

I went out into the living room.

The clock on the wall said it was four A.M. The house felt all weird and dead. The Sheetrock seemed to go on forever. Over by the TV there was this chocolate-icing handprint that had been on the wall since I was little. It was Welton's and he made it when he was like nine years old or something and my mom always liked it so she never cleaned it off the wall. I was suddenly terrified that Aunt Ricky was going to paint over it, so what I did was I went into the kitchen, grabbed a hammer and nail out of the toolbox below the sink, went back out into the living room, and hammered the nail into the wall, right above Welton's chocolate-icing handprint. Then I took my shirt off, which was just a regular white T-shirt with a few ketchup stains, and I hung it on the nail. What was this handprint, anyway? Was it some sort of weird warning of things to come? Was my brother giving us a sign, like, *I'm going to press right through these walls if I don't get the fuck out of here,* or something like that?

Soon Aunt Ricky would paint over all of these beautiful imperfections. The Nugent house was turning into some construction-paper cutout of a house. Inside there were a few stick figures modeled out of pipe cleaners and Scotch tape.

I opened the door to my mom's hospice room. The carpet had been replaced, and they had paneled over the walls. In this new bed that I had never seen before, my aunt Ricky was sleeping like some jungle beast that had survived a great hunt. Her mouth was sagging open. Her breathing sounded like furniture being dragged across the floor. I just stood there watching her for a moment. It was four A.M. and I was totally lost in my own house.

"We didn't have a dog!" I yelled. My own voice shocked me.

"Wha?" Aunt Ricky replied, waking a little. Her

nightgown was stained with these like *continents* of night sweat.

"Steven," she said, all wheezy and disoriented, "is that you, honey?"

"We never had a fucking dog!" I screamed.

At the time I honestly had no idea where this sentence came from. Now I realize that I was referring to what my mom had written on that piece of paper — that whole part about giving her dog a pat on the head.

I could hear Welton playing some PlayStation II snowboarding game down in the basement. The game was taunting him, going, "You're so lame!" over and over again. I imagined him staring at the graphics, not playing at all, trying to turn himself into the digital image of the snowboarder on the screen.

"Are you hungry, Steven?" Aunt Ricky asked. "Would you like a snack?"

That's when I started barking.

"Woof," I said. "Woof, woof."

At first, the barking came out the way it sounds when it is written in a book, literally like "woof, woof," but then it turned all carnivorous and savage, like I had rabies or whatever.

"Horf, horf," I screamed. "Horf-horf! *Ruff-ruff-horf. Horf-horf-ruff-horf-ruff. Woof-woof-horf.*"

I heard a door close and then my dad was in the

room. He was wearing this light-blue terry-cloth housecoat that was probably thirty years old. His shins were all white and hairless. The weird thing was that he had shaved and his hair was combed. I almost didn't even recognize him.

I stopped barking.

He said, "Barking's for dogs, Steven."

His voice was all weird and firm. Like he'd learned it at some seminar or like at Dad Camp or someplace. It was the first thing he had said to me since I'd left home.

"Dogs aren't allowed in the house," he added.

Aunt Ricky had propped herself up in the bed. In the four A.M. light, her wooden crucifix looked sort of like a weapon. Based on the expression on her face, she seemed pretty amazed.

It almost seemed like my dad had gone away and someone else had taken his place. For some reason, he still couldn't look at me. His eyes caught something on the wall and his hand rose up slowly and sort of caressed the grooves in the paneling. I walked past him and out into the hallway.

On my way back to my room, I came upon Welton, standing next to my bedroom door. He had come up from the basement, and he looked totally spooked. He was naked, and he was sort of hunched over, clutching his back. His nudity seemed sad yet weirdly profound

283

at the same time. It was like he knew some great, unbearable truth. His pupils were bigger than ever. He was obviously gone on Klonopin or Nembutal or whatever drug he and Dantly had experimented with that week.

"You okay, Welton?" I asked, but my question didn't register.

"Lincoln was a better president, Steve," he said.

He was basically meat with a voice.

"Better than who?" I asked.

He said, "Better than Washington."

"Oh," I replied.

He added, "You can tell 'cause of the pictures. His beard and stuff."

Then he took my face in his hands and kissed me on the lips. His mouth was cold and dry. For a moment he stared into my eyes but nothing more was said.

He is handsome, I remember thinking. *He is way more handsome than I will ever be.*

After he kissed me, he turned and headed back down to the basement.

29

The next morning I woke up starving.

After I used the eye drops that Dr. Black had pre-scribed, for some reason I urinated sitting down and I just stayed there on the toilet seat for a while. I had no idea what my plans were. If the calendar was right, I would be starting back at the gifted school in less than a week. So many things had gone wrong. My mom had died. I'd nearly poked my eye out. I'd never made it to that creative writing class over at Carroll High School. It felt like the summer had been a terrible mistake.

I could hear Welton's TV in the basement. It was on some game show and the volume was up a little louder than normal.

There was a knock on the front door. I walked through the living room and opened the door. Dantly stood on the other side of the entrance. He was naked from the chest up and his tattoos were all prolific and evil-looking. His nipples were pierced, too, and the light behind him made a weird halo around his body. The Skylark was idling in the driveway, smoke hurling from all sides.

"Hey, dude," he said.

His voice sounded cut in half. His shoulders were so slumped, they looked like they'd been wrenched from their sockets. His stomach was all tense and ripped with muscles. I thought for a minute that maybe he'd been in some sort of accident and he was in shock.

"Welton home?" he asked, hugging his shoulders. He couldn't really stand still very well and his tattoos sort of danced around all blue and serpentine.

"He's down in the basement," I said.

"Can you like get him for me?"

I went, "You can go down there."

He said, "I'm not walkin' too good, bra," and almost fell, but he used our mailbox to keep himself up. "We got into some heavy shit last night," he added.

"What happened?"

"Let's just say things got pretty dark."

I thought he was going to vomit in our mailbox—I really did.

"I'll be right back," I said, leaving Dantly at the doorway.

Down in the basement, Welton's door was three-quarters open. In his room *The Price Is Right* was on full volume. The Showcase Showdown music was blaring, and the studio audience was losing their minds. My brother's room was a cyclone of laundry and compact disc jewel boxes and warped and ketchup-stained paper plates. There were broken things and melted things and stains that couldn't be named. His computer screen was frozen on the Sims logo. His stereo had been turned down but a CD was spinning quietly. It was that Bottomside song "Forty Holes and Forty Goals." I turned the TV off and the music played.

> *there's a hole*
> *in my head*
> *there's a hole*
> *in my pocket*
> *there's a hole*
> *in the floor*
> *there's a hole*
> *in the door*
> *i'm gonna find it*
> *i'm gonna fill it*
> *there's a hole*

After the song ended, I pressed *stop* and turned the stereo off.

I turned around and there he was.

He'd hanged himself from a coat hook at the top of the door. He'd used one of my dad's old Marine Corps ties. He was nude and strange colors had settled into half of his face. Like blueberries and avocados.

He was sort of kneeling.

Like he was praying or planting grass.

His testicles had swelled really large, and his penis was sort of half-erect. The weirdest thing about it all, though, was that he had defecated on the floor.

For some reason I opened Welton's mouth. I don't know what I was looking for, maybe something miraculous like a baby bird or a gold coin.

I just stared at him for a moment.

"Hey," I remember hearing my voice say.

He had this totally awestruck expression on his face, almost like he was laughing, like someone had said something incredibly funny before he knotted the tie and dropped to his knees.

I said, "Everything's gonna be okay, okay?"

His eyes were sort of blank and agreeable.

Then I closed his door, which was actually really heavy, and headed back upstairs.

Dantly was still holding on to our mailbox for dear life. His Skylark was spewing monoxide all over the neighborhood.

"He's not down there," I said.

Dantly said, "He's not?" and the way he said it was like he was the victim of some horrible injustice.

I shook my head no.

"Well, where *is* the fucker?" he asked.

"Somewhere else," I said.

He said, "Somewhere *else?*"

I said, "Yeah, somewhere else."

"Where the fuck is *that,* bra?" he asked.

I couldn't answer and I wasn't crying, and these were the two thoughts that were colliding in my skull like enemy birds.

Then Dantly said, "Hey, man, what's your name again?"

I was like, "My *name?*"

"Yeah, your name, bra."

"It's Steve," I said.

"Steve—right, right. Sorry, man." Then he asked, "Do you know where Welton-I-Dealt-One keeps his stash?"

I said, "What stash?"

"His pills."

We went around to the backyard, and I dug up the spot where I had been stashing their pills in the "Itty-Bitty Pharmacy" Mason jar. I scooped up the dirt with my fingers and then Dantly joined me enthusiastically, almost athletically. He was suddenly wide-awake sober.

After we unearthed the jar, I handed it to him and he stared at the assortment of pills as if they were miraculous candies made especially for the deliverance of his warped soul.

"Golden," he said, grinning his head off.

His teeth looked glued on.

His eyes looked like marbles.

Then he said it again: "Golden."

And then he turned and left.

Dantly's bare back was the last thing about him that I remember. It was thin and muscular and zitless. A slightly tan, perfectly symmetrical back. A foot-long dragon sort of dived down between his shoulder blades. It was the back of a kung-fu hero.

A minute later I could hear his car door close and the Skylark pull away down the street.

I sat in the backyard for a long time. Sort of like I was at a picnic. Like there were hot dogs coming. Hot dogs and potato salad or whatever. The grass was hard and starting to lose its color. The sky was so blue it hurt to look at. The last few blackbirds were trying to nip at worms and other bugs that had already bored farther into the hard, cold earth.

It suddenly felt like the fall, and my only brother was dead.

30

At Welton's funeral, my cousin Grace wanted to see my eye.

"Show me," she said, sitting down next to me in the pew. "Come on."

But I wouldn't pull back the shield. I just shook my head and sat there.

St. Rose's was pretty depressing that morning, but there was some nice colored sunlight passing through the stained-glass windows and it felt sort of peaceful to just sit.

"I'm sorry about Welton," Grace said. And I think she sincerely was—I really do. And she is by far the prettiest girl in the whole extended family. She's eighteen now and at Drake studying premed.

"Are you gonna be okay?" she asked. She was nice—she really was.

I nodded and just kept looking at that sunlight.

When she was about to get up from the pew, I grabbed her by the shoulders and kissed her on the lips. I tried to open my mouth, too, so she was really shocked.

"That's wrong, Steve," she said. "That's so wrong."

I don't even know why I did that. I had no idea it was going to happen.

Then she got up and left the church. I'll probably never see her again, but I'm sure she's doing great at Drake.

After the funeral, I sat on the toilet for about two hours. Everyone else was at Aunt Ricky's bowling outing. Nothing like Galaxy Lanes to keep your spirits up.

On the toilet seat, I read an old greyhound racing program I'd kept from the spring season. I looked through it for a while, studying all the dogs, their weights and kennel positions, the different parks they'd been racing at, their most recent finishes.

In the back of the program, there was this ad for a dog track down in Florida. It was for Greyhound Park in Daytona Beach. There were races seven days a week, matinees on Saturday and Sunday, and the park was open twelve months a year. There was a picture of eight dogs fighting for the first curve, their snouts muzzled, their eyes all desperate and hellish. In a box at the bottom of this page there was an ad for Greyhound buses:

I went back down to Welton's room. His absence was like something hitting you in the back of the head. The door had been removed from the hinges.

There's this old cigar box that Welton used to keep in the back of the shelf of his closet. I knew he hid his extra money there, so I opened the door and helped myself to $327. It was mostly tens and twenties. Who knows where it came from. He'd probably made most of it selling drugs in the parking lot of Taco John's. I knew it was theft, but I didn't care about it at the time. Now I sort of feel bad about taking his money, even though he had no way of using it.

After I stuffed the knot of bills in the back pocket of my brown suit slacks, I sat in front of Welton's computer. It was a Gateway that my mom had bought him for Christmas a few years before, when he was still interested in stuff. He mostly used it to play Sims— Myst before that—and surf the Net. He and Dantly were always trying to find underground drug-dealing websites and porn pages. I wasn't all that versed in surfing the web, but I knew how to key in an address. After the computer fired up, I double-clicked on Internet Explorer and typed in the Greyhound Bus website. After I clicked on schedules, it told me that there was a bus leaving from the Rialto Inn, 200 Main Street, downtown Foote, at 3:20 P.M. To get to Daytona Beach, it would take me one day, fifteen hours, and ten minutes. A one-way fare would cost me $138. I would arrive at 5:30 A.M., just in time to catch a fresh Florida sunrise. That gave me about two hours to get to the Rialto Inn.

I walked upstairs and repacked my dad's old Marine Corps bag. I kept it simple. I packed a T-shirt or two, a pair of running shoes, a week's worth of underwear, a few pairs of socks, some medical tape, an extra optical shield, and the drops for my eye.

I was still wearing the brown suit that I'd worn to the funeral, and I didn't bother changing. I even kept the tie on.

When I left the house, the sky was huge and cloudless and I didn't look back once.

31

While crossing the bridge to Foote I got honked at by several cars. They love trying to embarrass pedestrians. It's usually pretty humiliating but I honestly didn't care. On my way to the Rialto Inn, I stopped in a magazine shop and bought a pack of Camel Lights and a few packs of gum.

I was hungry so I decided to stop in at Jack Palomino's. There were still all of those stupid movie posters plastered everywhere and the place smelled like mayonnaise.

Inside there were these three loners staring into their coffee cups. They were all sitting at separate booths and they seemed somehow similarly troubled. That same waitress with the knee braces was on duty.

"You again?" she said.

"I just want a hot dog," I pleaded.

We stared at each other for a moment, and she must have picked up on my desperate vibe because she pointed to a booth.

"You fuck around and I'm callin' the cops," she said.
I sat.

I had a little over an hour to kill. I figured I'd eat and make my way to the Rialto Inn, buy my bus ticket, and hang out in the lobby.

"Steve," a voice rang out. I turned to my right. It was June. Her eyes were all warm and smiley. Her pickle shirt had been replaced by a Carolina-blue hooded sweatshirt that featured a picture of that Spice Girl who's married to the famous soccer player. Her bangs had been cut and she looked at least two years younger.

I said, "Hey, June."

She was smiling so hard it made her teeth look huge. I never realized how many teeth she had.

She said, "Nice threads."

I said, "Thanks," and undid the knot in my tie.

"What happened to your eye?" she asked.

"It's a long story," I said, touching my shield.

"Are you blind?"

"I was for a few days."

"Did you get shot?"

"No," I said. "I sort of fell."

"Can I see it?"

"Not yet. It's pretty gross."

"This old man who lives on my street is blind," June

said. "He's got this dog that can like drive a car and read the newspaper and stuff. You should get a dog."

"Maybe I will. How have you been?"

"Okay," she said. "I quit smokin'."

"Good for you."

"Yeah. I had this dream that I spit up a roach. You should quit, too, or you'll croak, you know."

"You're probably right."

June said, "Why you all dressed up?"

"I was at a funeral," I said.

"Who died?"

"My brother."

"Oh," she said. "How old was he?"

"Seventeen."

"Was he sick?"

"He hanged himself with a necktie."

"Oh," she said. "Sorry."

I nodded and sort of played with my silverware ensemble.

To June, somebody dying was just another mild disappointment, like losing a quarter or failing to evade a spit bath. She'd already seen too much stuff.

I said, "Who cut your hair?"

"My mom. I wanted her to cut it all off but she wouldn't do it."

"Looks good."

She was like, "Yeah." Then she sniffed and said, "After you eat your hot dog, you wanna go see a movie with me? They got this one playin' about a pig."

I said, "I can't, June, but thanks."

"How come?"

"Because I'm leaving."

"Where you goin'?"

"Florida."

She went, "No, you ain't."

"My bus leaves in an hour. From the Rialto Inn. As soon as I finish eating, I'm outta here."

June slid into my booth, opposite me.

"Can I go with you?" she asked.

"I don't think your mom would be too happy about that."

"She won't care," she said. "She's with Eljay, anyway."

I said, "Where are they?"

"This place called Toronto, Canada. They said they'd be back three days ago, but they ain't back. I got a hundred bucks."

I guzzled the ice water that had somehow materialized at my table.

"You ever been to Florida before?" I asked.

"No. But I seen it on a map. It's yellow, right?"

"Yeah," I said. "It's yellow."

"'Cause of all the vitamins and sunshine they got down there."

The waitress arrived with my hot dog and Coke. I cut the hot dog in half and gave one end to June, who took it and ate it in about two bites. I pushed my Coke across to her, and she swallowed a mouthful.

I said, "You need to eat more."

She said, "I eat," and took another gulp of my Coke.

When we finished, I paid the check and June and I left the diner. The waitress sort of stared at me cock-eyed when I walked through the front door. Maybe it's because I tipped her way too much. I think I left her like a twenty-dollar bill or something.

Outside, the air was crisp and metallic-tasting, and downtown Foote seemed to be somehow asleep. June and I walked up the hill toward Main Street. We didn't talk, and during our silence she performed a series of kung-fu moves whose perfection I will never be able to re-create with words so I won't bother trying. One of her victims was a mailbox. Another was a parking meter.

"You warm enough?" I asked as we approached the Rialto Inn.

"I'm like a lizard," she said. "I don't get cold."

Our bus was parked in front of the hotel, and it looked sort of indifferent but somehow promising at the same time.

We went into the Rialto Inn and bought our tickets from a woman at the front desk. June's ticket cost seventy dollars. She produced a crinkled hundred-dollar bill from her sock and gave me her change.

"You can handle the money from now on," she said. I shoved her change in my pocket. It was weird because she didn't seem happy or sad. She just seemed sort of ready for whatever would come next.

The woman behind the counter told us that the bus was now boarding and for some reason felt the need to wish us luck.

"Good luck," she said, and went back to work.

When we boarded, this old black guy with electric hair took our tickets. He was the driver and he said it would be a few minutes before we left. His voice was all Southern-sounding and sleepy.

There were others on the bus, too: old people, young people, mothers with their sleeping children, a lonely old man with this tweed Bing Crosby hat. There was a college couple in the back who had so many suitcases you would've thought they were being paid to transport someone else's life to another city. It seemed like they'd all been on this bus for days, maybe even weeks.

We found two empty seats near the back. You could smell the urine fumes from the bathroom pretty strong, but I didn't care. I put my dad's Marine Corps bag in the overhead rack and took the window seat. June sat next to me and pinched my arm.

The bus driver closed the door and made some general announcement about all the cities that lay ahead: Davenport, Chicago, South Bend, Toledo, Columbus, Charleston, Wytheville, Winston-Salem, Augusta, Savannah, Waycross, Jacksonville, Gainesville, and Daytona Beach.

The driver also informed us that the bathroom was at the rear of the bus and that there would be no smoking or drinking of alcohol and that he would be making announcements along the way indicating where we'd be stopping for cigarette and meal breaks.

One day, fifteen hours, and ten minutes later, we'd arrive in Daytona Beach.

Then the engine started and the door closed and we started moving.

"Here we go," June said.

Through my window, Foote looked strange and silvery. Though I couldn't tell you for sure, I'd like to believe that the leaves were starting to turn. It was probably too early in the fall for that, but I'd still like to believe it.

The bus passed silently though the streets of downtown Foote, turned south on the highway, and began its journey toward Davenport. June was asleep on my shoulder. Her mouth was half-open and her chin was sort of damp and gluey-looking.

As we moved south on the highway, the strip malls were replaced by silos and grain elevators and other solemn-looking agricultural monoliths. The endless black fields were all scarred and lifeless-looking.

At some point it got cloudy.

It's weird—you look away for a few minutes and there they are: big gray clouds.

A little while later it started to rain.

32

So you're probably wondering how I wound up in the middle of Michigan at this place Burnstone Grove if I was on a Greyhound bus heading for Daytona Beach.

June had been sleeping most of the way, her head still on my shoulder, when we pulled into the Hinsdale Oasis rest stop. While the bus was parking, I sort of adjusted my shield a little because the medical tape was sort of losing its stickiness. When I took it off, everything on the right side was missing. I closed my left eye, keeping my right one open, and the world was suddenly black. I put the shield back on and went into the Oasis with June, hoping my sight would somehow miraculously return by the time we got inside.

In the bathroom of the Wendy's, I pulled my shield away again and everything was still missing on the right side so I knew something was seriously wrong. It was pretty scary and I almost fainted, but that black bus driver with the electric hair was in there with me and he helped me stand.

"You okay, partner?" he asked.

"It's my eye," I explained. "I just got out of the hospital and it's giving me some problems."

"Do you need medical attention?"

"No," I said. "I'm okay."

"You sure?"

"I'm sure," I said.

"I can call an ambulance, if you want."

"I better wait," I said. "I don't want to freak my little sister out. We haven't seen our mother in a long time and she's waiting for us down in Daytona Beach."

I don't know why I started lying like that. And it didn't even make sense that I brought up our fake mother. I guess the blindness thing was suddenly making me really nervous.

I put some drops in my eye, retaped my shield, and left the bathroom.

In the Wendy's dining area, June was sitting at a table, sort of swiveling her chair back and forth.

"What's wrong?" she asked. She was eating a Frosty and a large order of French fries.

"My eye's bothering me," I told her. "But I'll be fine."

"You should eat," she said.

"I'm not hungry. I'll probably eat the next time we stop."

"So what are we gonna do down in Florida?" she asked, eating her fries.

"I don't know," I said. "Stuff, I guess. It'll be fun."

"Maybe we could like buy a bungalow or something."

"Maybe," I said.

When we got to South Bend, Indiana, the bus pulled into the local Greyhound station to pick up passengers. My eye was really starting to freak me out. June was sound asleep again. I was going to go talk to that black guy with the electric hair about getting myself to a hospital, but I couldn't find him anywhere. A few minutes later, a new driver took the wheel. He was this old white guy with a leathery face. He sat down for a minute, put some of his personal belongings down, adjusted his seat, and then got back off the bus.

I looked at June for a second, and then I reached into my pocket, pulled out $135, and slid it into the front pocket of her hooded sweatshirt. Then I started to cry, but I didn't want to make any sound and the pressure was making my eye hurt like crazy so I made myself stop. I grabbed my dad's old Marine Corps bag and got off the bus while June was still sleeping.

I know it was wrong of me to leave June on that bus—I really do. I have no idea if she ever made it all the way down to Florida or what might have happened to her. I'll probably go to hell for it.

Sometimes I wonder if she met someone who was in better shape than I was and that maybe that person took a special interest in her and helped her find a new life. Or maybe she took the bus all the way back to Foote.

What I did after I saw the bus pull away was I walked up to this Hispanic woman who was working at this parking garage and asked her if she could point me to the nearest hospital. She said she didn't know where the hospital was, but that she would call an ambulance for me. For some reason, the idea of being picked up by an ambulance really freaked me out, so what I did was I went back to the Greyhound station and bought a ticket back to Foote.

I had to kill a few hours before the bus left, so I just sort of sat in one of those chairs with the portable black-and-white TVs, fed quarters into it, and watched sitcoms with my left eye.

So I won't bore you with details about the bus ride back to Foote and how I walked all the way home from the Rialto Inn and how I sat under that sycamore tree in our front yard for like four hours before my aunt Ricky came outside and how she had already gotten all this information about Burnstone Grove and how she sat there with her big flabby legs tucked under her and talked to me about the whole recovery thing for like two hours and about how it would help me and how she had had a few friends from Illinois who had sent their kids there, how one of them had been addicted to crystal meth and how she wound up finishing high school and getting more involved with her church and how it really helped her feel better about things. Aunt Ricky said some of the money from my mom's will would pay for it and that it would probably only be for a couple of months.

I was just sort of nodding along and staring at her wooden crucifix with my left eye and trying to pretend that I wasn't blind.

A week later, after a few visits to Dr. Black at Medical Associates confirmed the permanent blindness in my right eye, Aunt Ricky helped me pack up my stuff and we loaded up the Fairmont and she drove me up to the middle of Michigan.

My dad didn't even say goodbye. I just walked right past him when I left. He was watching TV with the sound turned down and sort of pulling at the little hairs on the backs of his hands.

33

So my new roommate got here the other day. His name is Ahmed and he's Pakistani. He grew up in Gary, Indiana, and he's really into hip-hop and Denis Johnson novels and he's a Gray Grouper like me. We have a good arrangement, because he pretty much just listens to his headphones and writes lyrics in this spiral notebook. He's really respectful of my stuff, and whenever Sinead comes over, he's cool and goes into the common area.

I don't know what he did to get here, but I'm sure he'll tell me soon enough. I think one of his parents got shot by a gang or something, but that's all I know and it's sort of a rumor.

The other day in group, this racist Red Grouper named Carl Voyce called him bin Laden.

"What do you guys think about all this stuff with our troops still being over in the Middle East?" Dr. Shays asked.

No one said anything for a minute and then Ahmed said, "I think it's wack."

Then Carl Voyce said, "Who asked you, bin Laden?"

Dr. Shays got pretty pissed off about that and called security and they immediately took Carl Voyce away.

The school part of Burnstone Grove starts in three days, and Sinead and I have talked about maybe moving to Chicago after we both get out of here and getting a place together. We are in love, and this is a masterful feeling.

"We could get a place in Bucktown," she said while we were eating in the cafeteria. It was New Year's Day, and the night before, we left the party early and went to her room and played cards and held each other a lot.

"Or Roscoe Village," she continued. "Roscoe Village is cool, too."

"Cool," I said.

They started giving her medication a few days ago. It's this stuff called Paxil, and it's supposed to help her be more emotionally consistent.

In counseling this morning, Mrs. Leene seemed pretty positive about my dad coming this afternoon.

"You excited?" she asked me.

"I think so," I said.

"I know he is," she said.

"I'm gonna introduce him to Sinead," I told her.

"He's looking forward to meeting her. . . . Just remember to take things slow, Steve."

So that's where I'm heading right now. There's this room called the Family Room where they let families meet in private, and I think my dad's there, waiting for me right now. I have to admit that I am looking forward to seeing him.

But before I head to the Family Room, I just have to say a few more things. I've been thinking about them a lot the past few days, and I really need to write them down. It's sort of this list I'm starting, so please bear with me. It's probably going to get a lot longer, but at least you'll see the beginning of it.

1. People are born and people die.
2. God moves meat around the world.
3. Parents get cancer and their ashes get stuffed into urns.
4. The urns get buried in holes.
5. Brothers break your heart.
6. Little kids are smarter than most people.
7. Some little kids die in hospital beds.
8. Greyhound buses are incredibly depressing and should be avoided at all costs.
9. Losing your virginity is sort of miraculous.
10. You have to deal with stuff on your own and that's all there is to it.